MISMATCHED UNDER THE MISTLETOE

JESS MICHAELS

For Michael. Best friends to lovers is my favorite real life fairytale.

And for all my readers. This was...a crazy year. I hope this happy story of two good people who deserve each other will make your season a little brighter. Happy Holidays!

The Twelve Days of Christmas

The first day of Christmas,
My true love sent to me
A partridge in a pear tree.

The second day of Christmas,
My true love sent to me
Two turtle doves and
A partridge in a pear tree.

The third day of Christmas,
My true love sent to me
Three French hens,
Two turtle doves and
A partridge in a pear tree.

The fourth day of Christmas,
My true love sent to me
Four colly birds,
Three French hens,
Two turtle doves and
A partridge in a pear tree.

The fifth day of Christmas,
My true love sent to me
Five gold rings,
Four colly birds,
Three French hens,
Two turtle doves and
A partridge in a pear tree.

The sixth day of Christmas,

My true love sent to me
Six geese a-laying,
Five gold rings,
Four colly birds,
Three French hens,
Two turtle doves and
A partridge in a pear tree.

The seventh day of Christmas,
My true love sent to me
Seven swans a-swimming,
Six geese a-laying
Five gold rings,
Four colly birds,
Three French hens,
Two turtle doves and
A partridge in a pear tree.

The eighth day of Christmas,
My true love sent to me
Eight maids a-milking,
Seven swans a-swimming,
Six geese a-laying,
Five gold rings,
Four colly birds,
Three French hens,
Two turtle doves and
A partridge in a pear tree.

The ninth day of Christmas,
My true love sent to me
Nine drummers drumming,
Eight maids a-milking,
Seven swans a-swimming,

Six geese a-laying,
Five gold rings,
Four colly birds,
Three French hens,
Two turtle doves and
A partridge in a pear tree.

The tenth day of Christmas,
My true love sent to me
Ten pipers piping,
Nine drummers drumming,
Eight maids a-milking,
Seven swans a-swimming,
Six geese a-laying,
Five gold rings,
Four colly birds,
Three French hens,
Two turtle doves and
A partridge in a pear tree.

The eleventh day of Christmas,
My true love sent to me
Eleven ladies dancing,
Ten pipers piping,
Nine drummers drumming,
Eight maids a-milking,
Seven swans a-swimming,
Six geese a-laying,
Five gold rings,
Four colly birds,
Three French hens,
Two turtle doves and
A partridge in a pear tree.

The twelfth day of Christmas,
My true love sent to me
Twelve fiddlers fiddling,
Eleven ladies dancing,
Ten pipers piping,
Nine drummers drumming,
Eight maids a-milking,
Seven swans a-swimming,
Six geese a-laying,
Five gold rings,
Four colly birds,
Three French hens,
Two turtle doves and
A partridge in a pear tree.

— ANONYMOUS

PROLOGUE

Spring 1804

"You cannot truly mean to *marry*." John Cavendish shook his head at his longest and truest friend, Andrew Rutledge. The party around them spun merrily on, but he hardly noticed it, so focused was he on this imperative moment. "You're barely one and twenty and have not even inherited your title. You must sow your oats a few years more before you surrender to the debutantes and mamas!"

Rutledge laughed. "My oats, as you put it, are sown, Cav. I will never have need to do that again."

Cav let out his breath in a frustrated sigh. "Great God, *please* don't wax poetic. Whoever this young lady is, she cannot deserve such gooey eyes and fluttering hands. Nor can I support her taking off the market one of the finest rakes ever to grace London."

"I think you are more concerned about losing your partner in trouble more than you are about my well-being," Rutledge said, but there was no heat or accusation to his tone. "I'm certain you won't be lacking friends at the brothels or gaming tables."

"You aren't planning on even going gaming anymore?" Cav burst out. "I really must meet this siren who has so bewitched my best and truest friend."

"And you shall, for she just entered the room." Rutledge lifted on the balls of his feet, seeking out someone in the crowd. Cav followed his friend's stare, looking from young lady to young lady and seeing none who would inspire such intense dedication and surrender within weeks of a first meeting.

He was about to make a snide comment about just that when the crowd parted a fraction and a woman stepped free from its jostling. Everything else fell away as she glided toward Cav. She had hair like corn silk, pulled back from a beautiful face with high cheekbones and full lips. Her eyes matched her gown, a Mediterranean blue that sparkled with delight as her mouth widened in a smile.

He couldn't breathe. It was the strangest thing. He'd been around dozens of beautiful women in his life. He'd danced with them and chatted with them and bedded more than a few. He'd never felt like this. As if a hand had pushed into his chest and constricted his heart. As if his world had been flipped on its head and now he had no idea how to right it.

It was a lightning bolt. The kind written about in books. And he realized, as she reached him, that he would never be the same.

"Rutledge!" she said with a delighted laugh.

Cav stared, the world winding down to half time as his best friend reached out and took the hand she offered. He lifted it to his lips and she blushed. She never took her eyes off Rutledge. He never took his eyes off her.

And the world that had been turned upside down a moment before felt destroyed as Cav realized *this* was the woman who had aroused such instant and intense adoration in Rutledge.

At least Cav understood now.

"Lady Emily, might I present my dearest friend John Cavendish. And Cav, this is Emily." Rutledge's chest puffed up with pride and delight. "She is the daughter of the Duke of Wolfsome, and somehow she has agreed to become *my* future bride."

Cav couldn't form words. How could one form words in a moment like this?

"Good evening," Lady Emily said when he did not say anything. She extended her hand toward him. "I've heard such wonderful things about you, Mr. Cavendish. I'm so pleased to make your acquaintance."

Cav blinked, fighting against the rising tide of emotion. He'd never been one to believe in love at first sight. How he wished that he'd never experienced it.

Rutledge cleared his throat, and his pointed glare was what Cav needed to jolt from his state of shock and awe.

"Lady Emily," he choked out as he bowed over the hand still waiting there for him. It was such a delicate hand. He engulfed it with his own. Wrong as it was, he wished she weren't wearing gloves in that moment, just so he could touch her. "I am pleased to meet you, as well."

That seemed to make Rutledge happy, for he stopped glaring and tucked Emily's hand into the crook of his arm. He grinned at Cav. "You *must* call him by his nickname, Emily. After all, he is my best friend, and what is mine is yours."

Cav had to fight not to physically recoil at that statement since Rutledge said it as he looked at him, not her. As if she could be *his*. Which was clearly and patently untrue. She looked up into Rutledge's face with pure adoration.

"I would only do so if Mr. Cavendish agreed to such a thing," she said with another of those fetching blushes.

"Of course," Cav managed to force past a suddenly dry throat. "After all, Rutledge is my best friend. And as he said, what is his is yours. I am at your service."

She smiled, and he could see how truly happy she was at the idea that they would all be fast friends. And they would be. Rutledge was more like a brother to Cav than a mere friend. If he had these strange, powerful feelings in this moment, surely he would master them.

"Well, I cannot wait for you two to get to know each other better,"

Rutledge said. "And now, Lady Emily, I would very much like to have the next dance, if your card is free."

"For you, it will always be free," she said, and her face lit up with joy and certainty.

Rutledge grinned again at Cav and then took her away, into the crowd, onto the dancefloor. As Cav watched his best friend dance with the remarkable woman he had chosen for his bride, he let his forced smile fall. They were happy together. And it hurt like a sword to the chest.

Mastering this sudden and powerful feeling might not be as easy as he hoped. So perhaps his better option was to push it down...down deep where horrible things like this belonged.

He would never act on it, that was all he knew. He was many things, not all of them good, but he would never allow himself to be the kind of man who would do that.

CHAPTER 1

Nine Years Later

L ady Emily Rutledge took the hand her driver offered and stepped down from her carriage on the walkway. She shook her head and looked up the stairway toward the front door. Outside, a footman swept the afternoon's dusting of snow away from the walkway, and she paused.

"Good afternoon, Arthur!"

The footman looked up from his work and gave her a smile. "Good afternoon, my lady. Almost finished here."

She nodded. "I see that."

"And how was the shopping?"

Emily laughed as she lifted the two satchels in her hands and motioned to the carriage, which was being unloaded as they spoke. "Productive. Thank you."

"Mr. Cavendish is here," the young man said.

Emily pursed her lips. Cav was always late to every appointment except the ones he took with her. It was a joke between them now, but on days like today she wished he hadn't changed that bad habit for her. "Oh, I know. I'm so late. Good afternoon, Arthur!"

As she scurried up the freshly swept steps, she heard the footman laughing after her. "Good afternoon, my lady."

She burst into the foyer to find her butler, Cringle, already waiting for her. She smiled as she handed over her packages, then her gloves, scarf and coat in rapid succession.

"Should these go in the gift room, my lady?" he asked, indicating the bags.

"Yes, those two and the ones outside." She gave him a conspiratorial look. "How long has Cav been waiting?"

"Mr. Cavendish has been in the parlor for a bit over a half an hour, my lady." He tilted his head.

She smothered another laugh. "Oh, I shall be railed upon for sure. Thank you, Cringle."

He nodded as he moved away to the room upstairs that Emily had long ago set aside for gifts and wrapping. She kept it well-stocked with items all year round, but never was it so packed as the weeks leading up to Christmas, when Emily filled it to capacity with gifts for her relatives, friends and servants. Just the thought of it now filled her with giddy anticipation of the reactions of those she cared about when they opened her perfect gift for them.

She threw open the parlor door to find Cav sitting on a settee beside the roaring fire. In the fraction of a moment it took for him to rise to his feet in greeting, a wash of emotion hit Emily in the chest. It had been five years since her husband died of a sudden fever, followed by both her parents.

Five years of heartbreak and mourning and loneliness. She had only truly begun to feel herself again in the last twelve months. But seeing Cav always brought Andrew back to her mind. Cav had been his best friend, after all.

He had become hers, too. When loss had become a constant companion, so had Cav.

She shook those thoughts aside as Cav got to his feet. He was a handsome man. Tall, broad shouldered, with dark blond curls that always looked just a bit mussed. Like he'd run his hands through them. Like someone else had done the same. Certainly plenty of someone else's had. The man had a certain reputation with the ladies.

"Emily," he said with a teasing arch of his brow and a quick flick of his head toward the clock on the mantel.

She laughed, pushing her thoughts away as she rushed to him and took his outstretched hands. "I know, I know!" she gasped. "I'm sorry to have kept you."

His gaze flickered over her face. The smile remained but something darker entered his eyes. She found herself glancing away from it. He often had that expression when he looked at her. Something a little...forlorn. She supposed she reminded him of Andrew, just as he reminded her.

"I am freezing," she said, releasing him and rushing to the sideboard to look at what had been brought for refreshments. "Did you pour yourself tea?"

He held up the cup from the table beside the settee. "And Cringle brought those cakes Mrs. Lisle makes this time of year. She must know I crave them."

"*Everyone* knows you crave them," she teased as she put sugar in her tea and then took a sip with a sigh of pleasure. "You make a very theatrical expression of it any time they are served."

"I know my audience," he said with a wink in her direction. "Mrs. Lisle loves my boisterous declarations, which allows me more cakes."

She shook her head. "You are hopeless. I don't even know why I invited you here."

He laughed, but he set his cup aside and took a long step toward her. The warmth of him hit her, the spicy scent that always accompanied his arrival a comfort.

"I'm not sure why you invited me either," he said. "But I'm sure I can ascertain the answer if you give me a moment to observe." He pressed a finger to his lips and looked her up and down. "You are happy."

She wrinkled her brow. "Don't sound so surprised by that fact. I'm a happy person, am I not?"

"You are, indeed. Practically bottled sunshine," he teased. "But today you are positively glowing. You are up to something."

"You do know me so well." Emily leaned closer. "Cav, I have had an idea. No, not just an idea, the *best* of ideas, and I need your help!"

Cav held her stare for a moment, then tilted his head back and laughed. The tendons in his neck flexed above his cravat as he did so. Emily blushed. She knew she was exuberant. She couldn't help it. Emotions were something she had never been able to hide. If she was joyful or excited, she showed it.

"All right, Emily. You have intrigued me. What is this idea?" he asked.

"Although we...lost Andrew five years ago," she began, and the smile on Cav's face fell slightly. He was truly the only one who felt the loss as keenly as she did. He had practically been Andrew's brother. She hastened to continue, "I have only returned to Society in the last eighteen months or so."

"Yes," he said, drawing out the word with a look of concern on his face. "And?"

"I've been doing something of a study of the gentleman and ladies of our acquaintance during that time," she said.

"I see," he said. "And what have you determined?"

"I have developed a few theories about matches that end up being successful to both partners." She smiled. "Not just financially or by linking important families, but by the happiness and affection the couple ultimately develops."

His mouth twitched. "Are you...in the market for happiness and affection in a match?"

She shook her head. "Gracious, no. I had both, you know I did. I am not in a position where I must marry, thanks to the financial protections Andrew put in place for me. I do not think I would *ever* be tempted to wed again."

He turned away and paced to the sideboard, where he fiddled with the bottles of liquor lined up along the top. "Then why make a study?"

"For other people," she burst out.

He stared at her, his expression utterly blank. "I don't understand."

She huffed out her breath. "I'm saying that *I* could successfully match couples who might not have ever thought of each other, if only I could seclude them together in the proper circumstances."

Cav leaned back. "Play...matchmaker."

Emily nodded. "*Yes*. And this is the perfect time of year to do so. The Christmas holidays are just around the corner, and there is romance in every snowflake and cheery red ribbon."

Cav smiled at her in that indulgent way he sometimes did when she was going on like this. "You should write one of those novels you insist on reading out loud to me in the winter."

"Oh, don't pretend that you don't love them," she said with a playful scowl. "I intend to have a party out at my estate in Crossfox and invite six ladies—and their chaperones, of course—and six gentlemen. Then I shall see if I can end the party with six very happy couples."

His eyes went wide and for what felt like an eternity he just stared at her. "A whole party to matchmake these poor unsuspecting people."

Emily pursed her lips in mild annoyance. "I know you are a resigned bachelor, Cav, and an unrepentant rake, but you act as if I intend to do something horrible to them."

"No. Just force them into each other's arms," Cav muttered. "And when do you propose to do this thing?"

"We will start the day after Christmas. Crossfox is so close to London, it isn't a difficult journey for any of those I intend to invite. I plan twelve days of merriment."

"Twelve days," Cav said. "Like the poem."

"Exactly." She clapped her hands together. "I know it doesn't line up exactly with the *real* twelve days of Christmas."

"Yes, one whole day off the true timeline. What will the scholars think?"

She laughed. "They will have to forgive me and say it's close enough. I have so many plans for each day and the fun that can be had with the poem."

"Wait, you are proceeding with the *theme* of the Twelve Days of Christmas?"

She tilted her head. "Of course! What could be more festive?"

"There are a great many birds in that poem, Emily," he said. "So, so many birds."

She folded her arms. "And I will manage them all. It will be enchanting."

He chuckled again. "Of course it will be. With you in charge, how could it be anything but?"

"Don't tease me," she said with a playful swat on his upper arm. "I sent out the invitations this morning before I went on my shopping excursion. And my estate staff is already readying themselves for the arrivals. Would you like to hear who I have in mind to attend?"

"I admit, I am curious," Cav let out a put-upon sigh as he motioned her to sit on the settee. He took the chair across from her and folded his arms across his broad chest. "Who are your victims?"

Emily frowned at the couching of the question, but then plowed on, undeterred. "First, the ladies. Miss Abigail Delafield."

He nodded. "Eldest daughter of the second son of Viscount Wayland. Only one left who is unmarried, yes?"

She nodded. "The Ladies Honoria and Prudence Mulberry."

"Twin daughters of the Earl of Mulberry." He pursed his lips. "A bit bluestocking, aren't they?"

Emily smiled. "Yes. They do like their books and tinkering with this and that. But they're very nice."

"I'm sure, but—"

Emily continued without listening to any further complaint. "Miss Bridget York."

"She's American."

"Her father is some kind of industrialist or some such thing." Emily nodded. "They moved to London two years ago, have more money than the king, it seems."

"And yet the lady remains unattached," Cav mused.

"Indeed. I think it is hard to break into a Society such as ours."

Emily shrugged. "Next is Lady Thea, daughter of the Earl of Beacham."

"The youngest of, Heaven preserve us, ten daughters, yes? I think her mother ran out of steam with her."

Emily nodded. "I've always thought the same thing."

"And that makes five. Who is the last lady?"

"Lady Hickson," she finished with a smile.

"But she is the widow of the Marquess of Hickson," Cav said with a shake of his head. "She was married."

Emily shrugged one shoulder. "Not very happily, by all accounts. And I've always sensed that Virginia perhaps wanted to find the right man the second time around."

Cav crossed one foot over his knee and steepled his fingers against it before he said, "Emily, I feel I must point out that every single lady on your list is considered a wallflower."

"Yes, I know. Not your type," she said, fighting the slight annoyance that accompanied the fact he knew so much about the women she'd listed. The man was who he was, of course. Except when he was around her. He was too respectful to dally in front of her, it seemed.

"No, I like women with a bit more season," he agreed. "But that isn't what I'm talking about. These women never dance, they rarely engage with men in conversation, they are teetering on the edge of old maidhood. With the exception of Lady Hickson, of course, who is a seemingly content widow with three cats."

"I know." Emily grinned. "Is it not genius? Six women on the fringes of Society. All lovely, sweet, kind and intelligent, but unable, thus far, to capture the right man."

"And you think you can do better?" Cav said softly. "Very well, who are the men you plan to help your ladies ensnare?"

"Mr. Wentworth Highsmith," she began, ticking the names off on her fingers. "The Earl of Allington, Viscount Weatherall, Mr. Adrian Powell, the Earl of Levenridge and Mr. Nathan Hayward."

Cav's eyes went very wide. "Those are all my friends. Or at least acquaintances."

She shrugged. "Rakes of a feather...speaking of birds."

He didn't smile, but folded his arms. "They *are* all rakes. Rogues of the highest order. Men with pasts as murky as spoiled water!"

Emily practically bounced in glee. "Yes. Isn't it marvelous? Think of it. Which matches are always the most successful, even if they are the least expected?" She didn't wait for Cav to give an answer. "A rake with a wallflower. I've watched several friends steeped in wallflower status catch men of questionable reputation and have the result turn out as one of love, respect and longevity. Rakes and wallflowers, *that* is my test."

Cav opened and shut his mouth like a fish a few times before he shook his head. "You are astounding."

"Is that a good thing?" she asked slowly.

After all these years, she could normally read Cav. She'd learned to do so as he'd been her rock and her ear and her...well, everything. But right now she couldn't tell if he thought her a true fool or that her plan wasn't one he could support.

He let out his breath slowly. "Always. But you said you require my help with this madcap plan of yours. What exactly do you need me to do?"

Suddenly Emily felt nervous, though she couldn't place why. Cav never made her nervous, and yet her hands had begun to shake and she shoved them into her lap so he wouldn't see. "Come to the gathering."

"To be witness to your matchmaking bird show," he said softly.

She laughed at his quip. "No. I need someone there who understands what I'm doing. Who knows the men as well as I know the women. Someone who can help push things along if need be."

He got up and walked across the room, stopping to turn at the mantel. He speared her with a look. "I see. A partner in crime, if you will."

There was something about the way he said it that brought her up short. She searched his handsome face, looking for why he was so hesitant. Was it her or the plan in general?

"A friend," she clarified gently. "You are my friend, Cav. My truest and dearest. I suppose it's silly, but when I think of doing something so fanciful, I only want you by my side as I do it."

He pursed his lips, but then he nodded. "Well, I cannot say no to you, can I? I never can. If you wish for me to join your party and your plan, I'll be there."

She rushed forward and grabbed for his hand, clutching it between her own. "I'm so happy!"

He pulled his hand away with a smile of his own. "Very good."

She smoothed her skirts and tried to stop her fluttering heart. The excitement over this whole endeavor was something she would have to work on controlling. She didn't want to be too obvious when it came to her quarry.

She sighed. "Now that it's all settled, I wonder what *you* are doing for Christmas Day."

"I'll join my grandfather," he said with a slightly sad smile. "As I do each year. My uncle will be there, and his wife and the cousins. We make merry and then everyone prods me about settling down. What about you?"

There was something gentler to that question. She knew why. While Cav had the extended family, she really didn't have many people. She had no siblings, her parents had both died right after Andrew did, adding more to her suffering during those awful days.

"Andrew's mother and his brother have invited me," she said. "They're very kind to keep me so close. I believe his brother will marry soon, and that will make me a dowager." She twisted her lips. "I'm happy for him, but when the real title is gone, it feels a little like…"

Cav completed the sentence. "Like Andrew is fully gone, too."

"Yes," she whispered, but then she shrugged away the pain that went with that thought. "Still, it will be jolly. And I will have my party to look forward to the next day, so that will help me get through the festivities."

"You could always join us," he suggested. "You know my grandfa-

13

ther thinks highly of you."

"The marquess is a delight, but no," she said. "I will allow you your family in peace."

Cav nodded, but she thought there was a flicker of disappointment in his stare. He glanced at the clock on her mantel and shook his head. "I'm afraid I must go now, to meet with the man, himself."

"Of course. Thank you again for coming, Cav," she said as they walked to the foyer together. "And for your indulgence in helping me."

As they waited for his horse, Cav looked down at her. His dark blue eyes held hers, focused entirely on her. How many ladies had gone faint at that look over the years? Even she felt a little flutter sometimes when he did that, even if she knew he felt nothing except friendship for her and she for him.

"If you call," he said, "I will answer. Good day, Emily."

"Good day, Cav," she said as he exited her foyer and swung up on the fine mount that had been brought for him. She watched him ride away into the cold. Soon enough she would see him again, this time as a partner in her plans.

She just hoped she would help the others find love in the countryside. Because this time of year, she had to believe everyone needed it a little more.

∽

"How was Lady Rutledge?" the Marquess of Comerford asked as he strode into his parlor where Cav had been waiting since his arrival.

Cav scowled at his grandfather, a man he looked very much like except for the graying hair and a scattering of wrinkles from a life well-lived. "And who says I was with Emily?"

The marquess snorted as he poured himself a drink. "You postponed our appointment today. The only reason you set our weekly meetings aside is for that lovely woman. So I *know* you were with her. You might as well not pretend otherwise."

"Nothing gets by you, does it?" Cav muttered as he flopped himself into the chair nearest the fire.

"I raised you since you were ten," his grandfather said as he, too, took a seat. "So the answer to that is no."

Cav shut his eyes. He adored his grandfather, who really *had* been more of a father over the years. Gruff though he might sometimes be, he loved Cav. He'd been a teacher, a friend, a confidante. He was lucky to have such a person in his life.

Of course that meant the marquess also knew him too well. "What did Lady Rutledge want?" he pressed.

Cav clenched his hands in his lap. "She invited me to a country party that will go until around Epiphany," he said. "It's a grand to-do, she's very excited about it. She wants my help."

"I see," his grandfather drawled. "And of course you cannot help but offer that assistance, no matter the cost to yourself."

"You should have seen her." Cav shook his head. "She was...*happy*. After the past few years, I am pleased to see it. Because she's my friend."

The marquess held his stare evenly. "And there's also the small fact that you are in love with her."

"Stop," Cav grunted as he got to his feet.

"I can't," the marquess insisted as he folded his arms and watched Cav pace the room. "I've watched you moon over that woman for nearly a decade. After Rutledge's death, after the proper amount of time had passed, I thought you might take your chance, but you didn't. You still haven't."

"Because she views me as a friend," Cav choked out. "She...needs a friend. And I...cannot say no to her. I've never been able to say no."

"So you break your own heart just to see her pleased for five minutes or five hours or five days," his grandfather grunted. "Don't misunderstand me, I like her. I've always liked her. She makes it impossible to do anything but." He got up and moved toward Cav. "But I more than like *you*, my boy. And I hate to see you hurt."

Cav felt his shoulders roll forward as defeat washed over him.

"How I feel doesn't matter, does it?"

His grandfather shook his head slowly. "If it doesn't matter, then you should move on. The Season will start in a few months. You are, as you always have been, a catch. And it is time for you to take a bride and begin to cement your legacy. You know that."

Cav bent his head. He would be thirty just before the next Season began. And though he wasn't titled, he did still have responsibilities. His grandfather, his uncle...they had been very patient with him, but he could see the firmness in the marquess's stare. The steel that would eventually come out and demand Cav move on, rather than suggest it.

"I know you're right," he said softly.

He expected his grandfather to smile, but instead the marquess looked...troubled at his acquiescence. As if he expected something more. Something different.

At last his grandfather turned away and paced back to the chair he'd abandoned. He sat back down. "Good. Very good. Well, you'll go to her party then, I suppose. And this will be your last chance if you want to press your friendship to something more."

Cav's knees actually went weak at that thought, and he gripped the mantel to steady himself. He hadn't thought of it in those terms before, but it was true. If he agreed to seriously pursue a match in the spring, that *did* mean this would be the last party he would attend where he would serve as Emily's confidante. It wouldn't be fair to any woman he would court or marry to carry on as close as they were. To keep being head over heels in love with her. He would have to find a way to distance himself for survival.

Was that what he wanted? To break away from Emily without ever trying to push for more? To keep his love wrapped away from her as a way to protect her? Protect himself?

He wasn't certain of the answer. But he would have to become so within the next few weeks. Because once he was at her party, the temptation of being near her was going to overwhelm him, as it always did. But was this the time to let her see the heart he hid? And what would she do if she saw it at last?

CHAPTER 2

A PARTRIDGE IN A PEAR TREE

E mily was all but quivering with anticipation as she watched a slow line of carriages glide through her gate at the end of the lane. The great manor her in-laws were kind enough to still allow her to use had grounds so vast that it was not a short distance from the gate to the house. But in a few moments, all her guests would reach her and she would begin the task of matching them with those she hoped would become the loves of their lives!

But who to match with whom? That was a question she had been pondering at length for weeks. A question that kept her heart and mind filled when sadness or loneliness crept in. A distraction, perhaps, but what was wrong with that?

She shook her head and refocused on matters at hand. Another question that plagued her was how to manage six couples falling madly in love *and* keep the holiday fun high. Each day of the gathering was carefully planned, of course, but she also wished to leave room for spontaneity. How could anyone sneak off to kiss in the orangery or dance in the moonlight if their every second was planned to the letter?

She sighed. She was getting ahead of herself, an old habit she recognized but sometimes had a difficult time breaking. For now she would focus on the present moment and enjoy her guests' arrival.

"You should calm yourself," Cav said as he joined her on the stair in her vigil on the approaching carriages. "You'll frighten them all away with that mad mask you're wearing."

She lifted her hands to her cheeks and found them hot. "Is it *very* mad?"

His smile gentled. "Of course not. You are never anything but lovely. But I do worry they'll suspect your intentions for them in a heartbeat."

Emily glanced up at him. Cav had arrived ahead of all the others that morning, all smiles and teasing and promises to help her in any way she needed. She'd been nervous beforehand, pacing and questioning herself about this plan. But once he was there at her side? The worries had faded away. His presence always did that in both the best and worst of times.

"Shush!" Emily admonished him playfully. "The first carriage will be stopping momentarily. You cannot reveal my plan to them or else it won't unfold naturally."

He looked out toward the gate with her. "There's still time to change your mind. Return the birds and hold a normal sort of party."

It was a tempting prospect, in truth. The entire idea of matchmaking, which had seemed so exciting when she originally hatched it, now felt a little more...overwhelming. To hold in her hands the potential futures of all these couples...what if she did something wrong? What if she caused someone pain, rather than happiness?

No, that wouldn't happen. She knew her theory of rakes and wallflowers was correct, and it would be proven in the next two weeks.

"What fun would that be?" she asked, and was pleased she sounded more certain about it then she felt.

He held her gaze for a moment, then shrugged. "I suppose you're right. Probably too late to cancel the fiddlers fiddling, at any rate."

"Yes, they have a strict policy," she teased. The tension felt like it was melting off her shoulders as they chatted. Exactly why she depended on this man.

He laughed. "Which reminds me—what are you doing today for the partridge in the pear tree? I see no flood of partridges to greet your guests with their calls or a grove of freshly planted pear trees lining your drive."

She glanced up at him from the corner of her eye. "We're having partridge with a poached pear sauce for our welcome supper, and a pear tart with vanilla cream sauce for the final course."

He pivoted to face her full on. "A feast! Is that all?"

"Isn't that enough?" she said with a laugh at the shock on his face.

"No." He arched a brow at her, which drew her attention to those dark blue eyes. They really were lovely; no wonder women always cooed over them. "I'll have you know I came out here for twelve days of birds shitting and squawking and I shall demand my money back if I don't receive that entertainment."

She pursed her lips. "You are the worst scoundrel, Cav, I swear it to be true."

"And yet you keep me around," he mused.

She knew he expected her to laugh, but instead something in her stomach felt a little...fluttery. She ignored it and said, "There will be plenty of excitement to come in the next few days. My more elaborate plans follow the simpler welcome tonight."

He nodded slowly. "Ah, I see. Don't want to scare off the victims."

The carriage that had entered the gate a few moments before was rumbling to a stop on the drive, and Emily placed her hands on Cav's chest to shove him back toward the house. A very firm, very warm chest, indeed. What was happening in her head? Was she so fluttery from this party that everything felt discombobulated and odd? That had to stop instantly.

"Go away, Mr. Cavendish," she said. "I will welcome my guests, myself."

He smiled as he pivoted toward the house. "Yes, best not make them confused as to why I'm here. There will be rumors about us, you know."

He was gone then, disappearing inside where she was certain he would warmly welcome her guests, despite his never-ending ribbing. She could depend on him.

However, his parting salvo wasn't that far off the mark. She knew people looked at them, with their close friendship, and wondered if there was more to it. Sometimes they wondered quite loudly. And often it was so hard to explain exactly what Cav meant to her without making the rumors all the louder.

"Lady Rutledge!"

Emily blinked and looked down at where the carriage was now open, her first guest already on the drive. It was the widow, Lady Hickson, and she was smiling up at Emily as the servants all bustled to unpack the carriage.

Emily shook off her odd thoughts as she came down the steps to greet her friend. She couldn't get swept up in worrying about what other people thought about her and Cav. She had work to do and now it had begun.

Within a few hours of his arrival, Cav found himself seated at a table that was all too familiar to him. In the years Andrew had lived, Cav had come to supper at Crossfox many times, and broken bread and laughed with his late friend and Emily. Sometimes those gatherings had been large parties like this one, where he could observe the couple without being noticed. Where he could more easily pretend that his feelings for Emily were just as brotherly as his feelings for Andrew had been.

Sometimes the party had been smaller, though. Sometimes it was just him with the two of them. Just him with his adoration for them both, and his jealousy that always reared up and had to be shoved back down with all his might. That action had become second nature eventually. And if Andrew noticed Cav's feelings...well, he had never said a word. It had certainly never damaged their friendship, for which Cav was eternally grateful.

Cav had joined Emily here a handful of times since Andrew's death, too, though always with others. It had never felt the same. That first year, Emily had hardly been able to stave off the weeping. She had roamed these halls, walked the ones in her home in London, and her pain had been unbearable. Yet Cav had borne it, because she needed him to do so. He'd walked with her, held her up, talked her through the unthinkable loss of her husband, followed swiftly by her beloved parents.

That she could survive such grief was something he respected. That she was finally coming back to herself, to the light, was more than a relief.

She laughed in that moment, drawing him back to the present from those painful memories, as if to prove the point she couldn't even know he was making. She gave the large room a sense of warmth with her mere existence. She was welcome and kindness embodied, and no one could feel less than embraced in her presence.

He was seated far down the table from her, but in some ways that position allowed him to watch her more closely. She was a butterfly, beautiful wings fluttering furiously as she chatted with her guests and nodded to the servants to move from one course to the next.

How many nights had he watched her like this, Andrew at his side, both in awe of her? Both loving her from afar as she brightened the room. And then, later, Cav would watch Andrew and Emily go up the stairs to their bed and he would...drink.

He hoped this party wouldn't lead to the same. Pining was unattractive. He was well aware of that.

The Earl of Allington was seated at his right, and before Cav could descend into even more maudlin musings, the earl elbowed him. "An interesting party, isn't it?"

Cav blinked and glanced again at Emily, looking over her gathering like a queen. She had not been subtle in pairing off the potential matches, despite all her talk of easing the group into her madcap scheme.

"Lady Rutledge *always* makes things interesting," Cav said carefully. "Do you remember that party she and Rutledge threw all those years ago with the snail races? The competition got ferocious."

Allington arched a brow at him. "I'm not talking about snail races or bygone times."

Cav knew exactly what he was talking about, but refused to admit it. "Then what?"

"You mean you haven't noticed the pattern in the seating chart?" Allington huffed out. When Cav remained silent, he grasped his arm. "Look again: gentleman, lady, gentleman, lady."

Cav glanced down the table as if he had not noticed this and shrugged. "Well, there are more ladies than gentlemen, to be fair."

"Because of the chaperones," Allington said with a roll of his eyes. "All of them sharpening their blades at the thought of landing one of the men in this room."

Cav chuckled at the look of desperation in his companion's eyes at even the thought of being caught in such a scheme. Poor Emily would have her work cut out for her if this was the reaction to a mere seating chart. And what could Cav do but try to help?

"But you and I are seated next to each other, and *I* am not a lady," he said. "Does that not ruin your hypothesis?"

A long glare was his friend's response, and then he sighed. "You are thick as thieves with Lady Rutledge and you are awfully quick to dismiss my observation. So I will ask you directly, man to man: is she playing matchmaker with this gathering?"

Cav shook his head with a stifled laugh. Poor Emily. She never did anything by half. It was her nature to run up to cliffs and jump off, arms outstretched and filled with belief she would either sprout wings or land safely away from any rocks below. It was one of her more charming qualities. But her exuberance meant she was not very good at subterfuge. Perhaps that was a way he could help her as they went along. God knew he had practice in lying.

"I'm sure she isn't doing something so bold," he lied. He leaned forward and glanced around Allington at Lady Thea. She was talking to her mother softly. "Would it be so bad if she were, though? She's placed you next to Lady Thea, and she is pretty enough. I've heard she's smart as a whip, too."

"I wouldn't know," Allington grunted. "She has hardly said two words to me tonight. Aside from a barely polite greeting, she only *glares* at me, as if she is offended by my very existence."

"Not an auspicious start," Cav muttered. "Perhaps Lady Rutledge will seat you beside someone else tomorrow. Until then, I am not the worst tablemate, am I?"

Allington gave another glare, this one more pointed than the last. "You can afford to be nonchalant about this. The lady doesn't seem to be arranging you beside anyone, does she? Don't you wonder why that is?"

As the final course was placed before them, Allington was distracted. Cav was just as happy, for he wasn't in the mood to discuss Emily's reasons not to match him. He knew what they were, after all. She saw him as a friend, nothing more. She expected him to always be there, holding out a hand to steady her when she stumbled. Offering a shoulder when she needed to weep.

He'd allowed himself to be placed in that position for so long that despite his reputation, he wasn't certain how to move from it. Either away from her or toward her.

He pushed the thoughts aside and the meal concluded shortly thereafter. The men and ladies parted company, the men heading to the billiard room with Cav for port and talk. He led them inside and poured the drinks as the conversation started.

"How long has Lady Rutledge been out of mourning?" Adrian Powell asked as he lined up the balls for a game.

Cav fought the urge to stiffen and finished handing out the drinks in silence. Of course no one else avoided that subject, as he did. It was bound to come up with her as hostess for this event.

"Several years," Lord Weatherall mused. "Though she's only been back in Society for...how long is it now, Cavendish?"

"Eighteen months," Cav said softly.

Nathan Hayward took a shot at the billiard table and swore as it bounced wrong. Then he straightened up. "Took Rutledge's passing hard, it seems. But tonight she was lively."

"And lovely," Weatherall said with a chuckle and a raised glass. "I wouldn't mind making merry chase with that one."

That resulted in a rousing laugh for the rest of the men. Cav fought to remain impassive. They weren't being disgusting or threatening. Rakes though they might be, none of the men Emily had invited to her soiree were cruel of heart. He would have intervened if that were the case.

But their casual implication that they'd like to pursue Emily still hit something...raw in him.

He'd stood by, quiet when he had longed to shout his feelings, patient when he'd wished to be bold because she needed a friend, not a man sniffing after her heels. But now these others were talking about her as if she were available.

And wasn't she? Enough time had passed, certainly, to make any move not untoward because of Andrew. What held Cav back?

Of course he knew the answer. Fear stopped him, just as it always had. Fear of rejection. Fear of damaging a friendship he held dear. Fear of hurting her...of breaking his own heart.

He was a coward when it came to her, that was all.

His grandfather's words a few weeks before rang in his ears as he sipped his port, that this was his last chance. Would he take it at long last? Or would this gathering end up being yet another regret on the pile of regrets when it came to Emily?

CHAPTER 3

TWO TURTLE DOVES

E mily looked over her guests milling on the drive in their winter cloaks and coats. They were lucky it was a mild afternoon, perfect for what she had in mind. She counted the group in her head and then frowned. They were missing one partygoer: Cav. He'd acted very strange after the gentlemen rejoined the ladies last night. Almost like he was avoiding her.

But that couldn't be true. Cav would not avoid her.

As if to prove the point, he strolled from the house in that moment and her breath caught. Never before had a man worn a greatcoat with such flair. It fitted his broad shoulders perfectly and the bottom hem swept across thick, muscular calves encased in shiny black boots.

"Forgive my tardiness," he called out, all friendliness and nothing awkward, so she must have been seeing things last night. "I forgot my gloves."

As he said the word, he tugged fawn gloves over his lean fingers. He winked at her as he passed, and she smiled at his cheek. She was glad whatever was troubling him had passed.

"Most excellent," she said. "Then we may begin. It's a wonderful day, and I thought a brisk walk around the estate would be bracing for all in attendance. But since today is our second day of Christmas, I thought we would stay close to the theme."

She was trying not to bounce as she whipped a handful of colorful ribbons from her pelisse pocket. "Did you know that turtle doves can see color?" she asked as she handed one ribbon out—carefully selected, of course—to each of the ladies in attendance. "And can be trained to come to a specific hue?"

She stepped back and lifted her hand as signal. There was a whooshing sound of wings from just around the corner of the house and then the turtle doves swept into sight. Six of them, rather than two, but each flying to the lady whose ribbon matched the one tied around its delicate leg.

The crowd oohed and ahhed, just as she had hoped. Though the twins, Ladies Honoria and Prudence, did squeal a little more in fright than pleasure.

"You will note the card for each lady around the leg of your new friend. Remove it and open it to see which gentleman will escort you around the estate today," Emily said with a quick glance toward Cav. He stood at the back of the crowd, arms folded, and when their gazes met, he gave a little flutter of soundless applause. A thrill worked through her at his impressed expression of surprise. It was hard to throw him off, and doing so flooded her with pride.

She refocused her attention on her victims. Damn, had she just thought of them as victims? Cav's ridiculous word. Her *guests*! They were opening their cards, laughing as they paired off, and then the birds flew away, back to their handler behind the house.

"Off you go, just down the path," Emily called out as they began to move away. "You'll see markers to guide your way!"

Eventually the last coupling walked away, the chaperones gathering as a group to follow, and that left her with Cav. He arched a brow at her. "Well played. Now where is your cloak?"

She glanced down at herself. Though she wore a spencer, it wouldn't be warm enough. "Oh, I am a goose," she said with a giggle. "I was so excited for my reveal of today's theme, I left it inside."

"Geese are Day Six," he called out as he hustled up the stairs. "Don't get ahead of yourself." He returned a moment later, her black cloak with the stunning red lining in his hands. He motioned her to put her back to him and she did. "My lady," he said.

He placed the cloak over her shoulders, and for a moment his hands rested there, warm even through the heavy woolen fabric. She had a sudden urge to lean back, rest against that broad chest. Let even more of his warmth seep into every part of her.

She blinked. What was she thinking? Why was she so aware of Cav and his presence? She staggered forward, nearly depositing herself off the steps. It was only that he caught her elbow and steadied her that kept her from making such an inelegant display.

"W-We should go," she stammered, refusing to look up at him. "The others will get too far ahead with our dawdling."

He stood there for a moment, long enough that she forced herself to meet his gaze. It was even and steady on hers, his expression one she could not read. Then he nodded and the intensity faded, her friend returned and the tightness in her chest relaxed a fraction.

"Of course." He swept out a hand. "After you."

They walked together in the same direction as the others had taken. Swiftly at first, but they quickly met up with the retreating backs of the others and she made herself slow down, take a breath, even though she couldn't seem to find a full one. What was wrong with her? She was acting like a schoolgirl.

She cleared her throat and broke what she could not rightly call a comfortable silence. "Do you think it is going well?"

He glanced down at her. "It has hardly begun, so it is hard to judge. No one has devolved into fisticuffs, so that may be the best we can hope for on Day Two of this endeavor."

She frowned. He was teasing her, as he often did, but in this moment what she was doing felt very serious. She shook her head. "Cav."

He cleared his throat. "The doves were a lovely trick. Turtle doves have such beautiful rainbow markings on their wings—the ribbons were the perfect touch."

"Thank you. Though it was really Mr. Jennings who trains the birds and was kind enough to allow me to borrow their talents for a few moments."

"They will be talking about it for years to come. I'd wager a few of the mamas might steal the idea for one of their parties." He winked at her. "Though likely not Countess Mulberry."

She had to laugh at that. "The twins *did* seem more terrified than pleased when two birds swooped down to land on their hands."

"I think Lady Honoria was trying to shake hers off," he said.

She stopped on the path with a gasp. "Was she? I didn't even notice."

"She leaned back so far I thought she was trying to detach her arm rather than untie the ribbon," he said.

She bent at the waist as laughter rocked her. "Well, birds are not for everyone. I feel terrible that they are going to have to endure so many. But it is for a good cause."

He motioned her to walk again, and she did. This time the silence was more comfortable, but it remained charged. "I know you have something to say," she said at last. "I can practically hear that mind of yours buzzing."

He cleared his throat. "I'm just realizing how truly invested you are in this endeavor, Emily. I thought it was a lark, one of your fantastical ideas, but it's more than that, isn't it?"

"Yes," she whispered.

"Why?" he asked.

She ignored him and kept walking. The rest of the party had gathered in the clearing where tables were set up and a spread of delightful winter delicacies awaited. A few more steps and she would be safe from Cav's watchful eyes and his questions that poked into the softer parts of her.

Places he likely shouldn't go, no matter how friendly they were.

"Emily," he said, his tone suddenly firmer. He caught her hand, and she was kept from going down the hill to her guests. She pivoted slowly and faced him. His blonde curls had been stirred by the light breeze as they walked, and she felt the strongest desire to reach up and smooth them. Her gaze flickered unexpectedly to his lips, a little darker in the cold air. Full, though. The kind of lips other women dreamed of kissing.

Not her. Other women.

"Why?" he asked, his voice suddenly lower, rougher.

She swallowed hard and looked down at the others milling about, some still in their original pairings, some broken off in other groups. She ought to be marking that, adding it to her notebook of what was working and what wasn't.

Instead she tried to find an answer for a man who knew her almost as well as she knew herself.

"I had love," she whispered, bent her head to look at the brown grass at her feet. "And like this grass, it died. But I know the power of it. The beauty of finding a person who completes your heart."

She looked up and expected Cav to have sympathy on his face. Understanding. That was his usual expression when they discussed the past, Andrew, what they had both lost.

Today, though, it was different. His expression was guarded, those full lips now pressed together as if he were...upset at the topic. His body was filled with tension, his fingers flexing open and shut at his side.

"You can't force that, though, Emily," he said softly. "I know that better than most. You can't make people love each other by marching them down to the clearing and giving them punch."

She wrinkled her brow. "I'm...not trying to *make* them. I just think everyone deserves love. Or at least a chance at it. Don't you believe that?"

"Yes," he said, his tone a little strangled.

She worried her lip. This exchange was troubling. Not what she had expected. She moved a step closer to him, perhaps too close. Certainly she felt too close now, though they'd been this close while dancing or when he helped her from a carriage. Why did this feel so different than those other times?

"What about you? Is there anyone you would like to..." Her tongue suddenly felt thick and she had to force the next words from her lips. "...match with?"

He held her stare for what felt like forever. Then he caught her hand in his and squeezed. "I'll take care of my own match, Emily. Now let's join them, shall we?"

He released her and walked off down the hill and into the crowd. She forced herself to move, to catch up.

Over the years, she had heard many people ask Cav about his intentions, his heart. He'd always laughed them off. But today he hadn't denied that there was some woman he was hoping to match with. Someone specific. Who was she? Was she here?

And why did that thought make her head spin and her knees go weak? Cavendish was her friend. She should be happy he was considering the future—it was troubling that he had never done so before.

Yet when she pictured this man wooing and wedding another woman, it wasn't joy for him that filled her being. It was something else, something darker. Something she had no place feeling.

So she pushed it away, tried to ignore it, and focused on the matches she already had planned. Cav couldn't be her problem. To make him so was courting a danger she had never realized existed.

CHAPTER 4

THREE FRENCH HENS

C av had always leaned into the cliché that a rake kept abed until the afternoon. It was one of the beliefs that made his world go 'round: stay out late, sleep all day. But today, on the third morning of Emily's party, he found himself wide awake before the sun. He'd dressed and paced and read and paced, but his troubles didn't fade. After all, he was in the usual room he took when he stayed at Crossfox. Six doors down from her room.

Just the knowledge that she was so close was enough to make him toss and turn and fantasize long into the night.

"And *this* is how you wake up hard as a rock," Cav muttered as he tossed the book he'd been unable to focus upon aside and stared out the window instead.

At present he truly hated himself. Hated that yesterday he'd touched her just a bit too long when he helped her with her cloak. Hated that she'd looked at his mouth and his heart leapt with hope. Hated that she'd asked who he wanted to woo and ruined any fantasy that she might be interested.

"You are an idiot," he said to himself.

"Me?"

He turned and stifled a sigh. Emily was standing at the parlor door. She was wearing *the* dark green gown, the one with the velvet ribbon around the edging and the beautifully stitched peacocks at the hem. A matching velvet ribbon was wound through her corn silk hair, and he had a desperate desire to tug it free and let the curls loose.

He blinked. "Of course not you," he said. "I didn't realize anyone else was up and moving yet."

She had not yet entered the room, which was odd. She was just standing there...staring at him. Why was she staring at him like that?

"Em?" he pressed.

She blinked and took a long step toward him. "Er, yes...no."

He wrinkled his brow. "What was that?"

"I'm sorry, it's been an odd day already," she said with a shake of her head. "I'm finding it difficult to focus. I believe we are the only two actually downstairs yet, but reports are that the others are beginning to stir and ready for the day."

"Day Three. If I'm not mistaken, a true love should bring to you—er, *them*—three French hens. I look forward to seeing what that will look like from your wonderful mind."

She bent her head and her gaze darted away from him. "For supper tonight we'll have coq au vin and I've drawn out the most adorable little hen nameplates." She lifted her gaze. "Would you like to see them?"

"Of course." He didn't have to force the smile despite how awkward this conversation was turning out to be. "I always love seeing your handiwork."

She blushed and held up a hand before she dashed from the parlor. He could easily imagine her next steps, rushing to her study down the hall, a pretty room that overlooked the garden. Her escritoire had been given to her by Rutledge in their second year of marriage. He'd insisted Cav come with him to pick it out. Rutledge had tried to choose some big, awful oak thing. Cav had steered him differently. He'd won.

And hearing her coo over that desk had kept him satisfied for six months afterward.

He blinked as she re-entered the room. "I only brought yours so I won't mix up the stack," she explained as she held out the folded sheet of heavy paper.

She had hand-drawn three French hens in the corner of the nameplate, pecking at unseen corn. Beautiful little sketches, and he was certain everyone at the table would be enchanted by them because she was a wonderful artist. In a different time, with a different life, perhaps she could have even been a professional.

But it wasn't the hens that made him keep staring. He and Emily had exchanged hundreds of letters over the years. Writing was the way of Society, after all, even if they were in the same city. But no one else in his acquaintance wrote his name like she did. The swirl of the C in Cavendish felt like a caress. It didn't make him proud, but he absolutely planned to take this nameplate once supper had ended. He'd add it to the chest of letters she'd written and drawings she'd made for him, and all the other keepsakes that marked their friendship over the years.

"Is it that awful?" she asked, both teasing and nervousness in her tone as she asked the question. "You're just staring at it."

He let himself meet her eyes. "It's beautiful. I love the way the one little hen is tilting her head, looking right at the person at the table."

She blushed. "Thank you. I only did that with yours. I thought you might like to make eye contact with a bird. That's what...you men sometimes call women birds, don't you?"

He chuckled. "Sometimes, yes. Well, then I see who you've matched me with for your grand experiment." He held up the card next to his face. "Do we suit?"

She giggled and snatched the card away. "You and your great love will have to get to know each other tonight. Until then, I will sequester her from your rakish charms."

"I will find a way, Lady Rutledge," he teased. "You shall not keep us apart."

Her gaze remained on his face for a moment, and to his surprise, something in the room shifted. He knew how to recognize it. Aside from the fact he'd been desperately in love with a woman he couldn't have for almost a decade, in every other way he was a true rake. He took lovers, he danced with ladies...all in a desperate attempt to find one who would make him forget the one before him...but no one had to know *that* small fact.

Still, with his experience, he understood when a woman was attracted to him. He recognized the tells of how her gaze might slip to his lips or her pupils might dilate or she might lean in a little toward him.

Emily swallowed hard, her gaze slipped to his lips, her pupils dilated and she leaned toward him a fraction. His stomach flipped. Was he seeing this because he so badly wanted to see it? Or was it real?

"So supper and nameplates," he choked out, trying to keep the conversation light so he wouldn't frighten her away from whatever was happening between them. "Is that all?"

She shook her head slightly, as if she were trying to shake off the same thing he'd felt spark between them. She stepped away. The spell was broken.

"Well, no," she said, and her mouth twitched with a smile. "There is one other thing. Would you like to see?"

"You look positively wicked, my lady," he said. "So yes."

She laughed as she motioned him to follow her and he did. They wound through the halls and down and out a back entrance that led directly into the garden. He stopped and stared, because a dozen footmen were bringing small covered cages to arrange beneath the guestrooms above.

"Emily, you aren't—"

She glanced over her shoulder with a smile and nodded. "Come on then!"

He followed her out into the garden and she grinned as she lifted a hand and then dropped it dramatically. The footmen uncovered and opened the cages, and the birds exited. They began to squawk and call and cock-a-doodle-doo, filling the air with screeching. At the windows above, faces began to appear. The other guests, looking down some with interest, some in horror and some with annoyance.

"They're French Hens," Emily said, covering her ears.

"They're cocks," he corrected her, shouting to be heard over the cacophony.

She shook her head like she didn't understand him, and he laughed as he grabbed her hand and pulled her away from the squawking. She wasn't wearing gloves and neither was he, and he reveled in the softness of her fingers in his. He couldn't help but stroke the ball of his thumb in that tender place where her thumb and forefinger met. Her hand squeezed tighter in his in response and he glanced down, but her expression hadn't changed.

They had to go halfway into the garden, through the hedge maze, before it was quiet enough that he could be heard. "Well, that's one way to wake your guests up."

"On French Hen Day, one must provide French hens," she said, though she looked back toward the house with a concerned expression.

"Except you didn't. Those are cocks," he repeated as he leaned forward. "Trust me, I know cocks."

Her mouth dropped open and she laughed. "Cav, you devil."

He was painfully aware of how close they were now. He could feel her warm breath in the brisk cold of the morning, brushing his chin, almost touching his lips. He had to stop himself from reaching for her, from tracing the line of her arm with his hand, from tugging her closer and molding her against him.

Her breath hitched, her pupils dilated again, and this time it wasn't something he could explain away or ignore. For the second time in a quarter of an hour, he felt that she...desired him. His world ground to a halt as he processed that realization.

This was *not* his heated imagination. This was not wanting something that wasn't there. Her hands trembled at her sides, she looked at his mouth, she leaned just a fraction closer. Everything about her said *kiss me, kiss me, please kiss me.*

He might have done so, he wanted desperately to do so, but she seemed to realize what she was doing. She staggered a long step away, her hands coming up to her lips.

"Thank you for your help," she rasped. "I-I should go inside. I should...I should go inside."

She pivoted and practically ran toward the house, leaving him to stare after her, stunned. Stunned and...thrilled. If she wanted him, even in some deep, dark corner of herself that she had never allowed free until now, until this moment...then he had a chance. Desire could be molded into something more. Surrender on a physical sphere might open the door for surrender in some other way.

His grandfather's words rang in his head again. He had never taken his shot with Emily. First because of Andrew. Later because of her grief and the threat it might cause to everything they'd become to one another. But now she was out of mourning. Now she was free. And he had to take this chance. Slowly, perhaps. Carefully.

He walked toward the house, toward the calling, squawking cocks that still raced around the yard beneath the windows, and he could not help the spring in his step. The chance he had longed for from the moment he'd first laid eyes on Emily was happening. And he wasn't going to walk away this time.

~

E mily's hands shook as she poured tea for the women in her party. The men had gone riding for the afternoon. A good thing because since that morning, she had felt...out of sorts. She couldn't place why.

God, that wasn't true. She knew exactly why. That moment in the garden with Cav was why. They'd been laughing and teasing as they always did, and then suddenly she'd looked up into his eyes and all she'd wanted to do was touch him. All she'd wanted was for him to touch her. Not as a friend. Not in a grazing fashion she could pretend away later.

She'd wanted him to claim her mouth with his. Hard and fast, until the cold in the air melted away and all that remained was the heat of him.

Had she thought of Cav in sexual terms over the years? Perhaps. Always fleeting, always pushed away. She'd had a few detailed dreams, as well. Especially in the last eighteen months or so. Dreams where he was in her bed...naked. Doing things she hadn't had done to her in years. She'd woken with her hand between her legs, sweating as her body shook with pleasure. Self-loathing always followed.

But those were secret fantasies! The garden had been something else entirely. That had been real. He was real. He was her friend. She couldn't...*want* him.

"Isn't that right, Lady Rutledge?"

Emily started as she realized Abigail Delafield was talking to her. The eldest daughter of the second son of the Earl of Wayland was a pretty woman, raven-haired and quick to smile. Emily had always enjoyed her company and couldn't understand why she'd never married. She was a catch by anyone's imagining.

"I'm sorry, I was woolgathering," she said, trying to focus. "What was that?"

Abigail smiled. "I was just saying that after the first few days of your Twelve Days of Christmas theme, I have to imagine we have much to look forward to."

Emily blinked. Though most in the room were smiling and nodding, a few of the ladies or their chaperones were whispering amongst themselves as if they were a little annoyed. And to be fair, the morning with the chickens had not gone exactly to plan. Who would have thought the cocks would squawk so much and try to fight?

"I do have plans, though I must admit wrangling birds is a bit more difficult than I imagined," she said. She shifted. She really should focus on her efforts rather than think only about Cav and whatever had transpired between them in the garden a few hours before. "Are you all enjoying yourselves? What do you think of the gentlemen?"

The ladies in the room exchanged glances and then the polite murmurs began. Emily frowned. Honestly, she'd pictured this entire endeavor going very differently. The birds were supposed to be docile, the ladies and gentlemen were supposed to take to each other immediately and Cav was supposed to be her support, not haunting her dreams.

But no, she couldn't be discouraged so swiftly. Tomorrow's display with the blackbirds was going to be beautiful, and she just needed to find the right matches for the ladies. As for Cav...

"The Earl of Allington was just telling me last night about his horses," she said, looking across the room toward the Mulberry twins. Everyone knew they adored horses, so perhaps this would spark their interest in the earl.

But it was Lady Thea, the daughter of the Earl of Beacham, who answered with a scowl. "Pompous arse that he is, I doubt he could seat a horse for more than five minutes."

That caused a gasp and an uncomfortable titter in the room. Emily shifted. She'd tried to place Allington and Thea together on the first night, after hearing they'd known each other in childhood. Who wasn't swept away by a romance seeded in youth? But she could see now she'd made a tactical error, for Thea clearly despised the earl. Worse, she was making everyone else question him.

She made a note to talk to Cav about the man later and changed the subject. "And Mr. Hayward was telling me some very interesting things about his work on steam engines. He tells me that rail is the future."

Bridget York, the American, sent a side glance to her mother before she said, "Ah, yet another man who can only speak of steam. I wonder if he can generate it?"

"Bridget!" her mother said in scandalized tones.

But it seemed not to trouble her daughter, because she only laughed as she went to freshen her tea.

Emily bent her head as the ladies changed the subject, and suddenly they were all discussing a book almost everyone had read. She had enjoyed the piece, as well, but she still found herself disappointed. She'd believed so thoroughly in her efforts here, and yet the ladies didn't seem as engrossed as she had hoped.

She would have to just try again. This was love, after all. She knew full well it was worth fighting for. She would just have to do it harder on their behalves. Her mind darted yet again to Cav's intense stare in the garden, but managed to push the memory away again.

That wasn't the same thing as what she was trying to create here for the ladies and gentlemen at her gathering. Cav was something else entirely, and she wasn't about to go analyzing it and creating a situation where one did not have to exist.

CHAPTER 5

FOUR COLLY BIRDS

W hy Emily had brought him here when she was just going to
repeatedly avoid him was the question on Cav's mind the
next day when the group as a whole stepped into the garden for their
next display in her Twelve Days of Christmas tableau. She was
standing with a group of the ladies, talking softly, and her aqua gaze
lifted to him. She blushed and looked away.

He hated this. Hated that something had shifted between them and
made her cower from him. Yet he also found hope in that change.
She'd never been so uncomfortable around him, never blushed and
darted her gaze to anything but him.

He arched a brow, challenging her, when she dared to peek at him
again. Her blush deepened, but then she said something to her guests
and moved across the garden in his direction. When she reached him,
she smiled.

"I'm very much looking forward to our next reveal," he said
in an attempt to break the discomfort between them, and to
remind her that he was her friend. "I'm certain it will be spectacular."

"I hope so," she mused, and glanced off with what appeared to be
worry. "I was thinking we'd begin by now. But I suppose that allows

me to ask you a question that has been plaguing my mind since yesterday."

He tensed. Was she about to bring up the subject of what had happened between them right in this very garden? "If I can help ease that mind, I'm happy to do so."

She looked over her shoulder, as if making sure no one else was able to hear her. Then she drew a deep breath and said, "Have you heard anything untoward about the Earl of Allington?"

He cocked his head. "Allington?" he repeated.

She nodded. "It seems Lady Thea is very much not...fond of him."

"She hates him," he corrected with a chuckle. "I saw them together the first night and he mentioned it, as well. I have no idea why."

"Do you think it is because he is...cruel in some way? Or the sort of man I ought not match with any of the ladies in our party?"

His shoulders relaxed. Of course, she was concerned with the well-being of the ladies in attendance. That was who Emily was. It was part of why he adored her.

He shook his head. "Rake though Lord Allington may be, I would never allow you to invite someone who was truly a villain. I've never seen him be untoward before and I would have told you if he had a cruel streak. Whatever is between him and Lady Thea is just that—between them. It seems to be a personal matter."

"You don't think he might be...privately terrible?" she whispered.

He wrinkled his brow. "I...suppose that is possible. We often don't know what is in another's mind or what happens behind closed doors. But I've known the man most of my life. I've observed him when he might not have known I was there. And he's never acted in a way that would give *me* pause, for what it's worth."

Emily practically sagged in relief. "I knew that to be true, of course. I can always depend on you. I only worried when she spoke of him in such strenuous terms. But if I keep them apart, I think I shall solve the problem."

"I don't know," he said. "Sometimes hate is awfully close to love."

Her eyes widened, but before she could respond to that statement, her butler, Cringle, approached, a look of concern on his face. "I'm sorry to intrude, my lady," he began, then leaned in and whispered something to Emily.

Cav watched as all the color drained from her face. "Not coming?" she repeated, her voice trembling slightly. "But...but he made the agreement. He took ten pounds for the presentation."

"I know, my lady. But that is what we've been told."

Emily glanced toward Cav, and her frustration was clear in those beautiful eyes. He reached for her and almost took her hand before he forced himself to grip his fingers at his side instead. "Trouble?"

She nodded. "I hired a local man to come and do a demonstration. He said he has trained ravens to fetch shiny buttons and dance on the air for the promise of cheese. I thought it would be charming, but... but it seems he is a charlatan and is not going to make it after all."

Cav's jaw set as her bottom lip began to tremble. Her upset increased, even as she fought to manage it. "Do you have another option for your four colly birds?" he asked gently.

"No. This seemed so jolly and interesting, I never thought about another plan." She glanced around at the milling crowd. They were already restless. "What will I do? I don't want to disappoint anyone. They expect colly birds."

She worked her lower lip with her teeth. An action he'd always found wildly distracting, but today he couldn't be mesmerized by it. Today it meant her pain and her worry. Those were things he only wished to ease.

He drew in a long breath and smiled at her. "You brought me here to assist you," he said. "And so I shall."

She tilted her head, but before she could ask him what his intentions were, before he could talk himself out of them, he strode away and jumped up on a bench beside the garden path.

"On the fourth day of Christmas, my true love sent to me four colly birds. And so I present to you Richard Jago's 'The Blackbirds.'"

He held Emily's gaze as he said it and the reaction he expected was the one she gave. After all, this was the poem she had recited over and over after Rutledge's death. The one he knew by heart because her voice had been the one to say it. And yet it was the way to both assist her with her troubles and allow him to reveal something of himself to her.

The words he was about to recite were also ones that meant the world to him. He could only hope she might catch the meaning of them when he spoke them to her here and now.

~

"The Blackbirds" had been a favorite poem of Emily's all her life. Not only was it passionate and romantic, but it was bitterly sad, since it ended with the mated birds being parted by the reckless shot of a hunter's rifle. How much she had clung to the bitter heartache after Andrew's death. How often had she repeated the poem out as Cav looked on, his own expression as broken as hers.

It had become *their* poem, in a way, something that celebrated what they'd lost. Cav had never been one to exhibit, though. He was not the man who had a few drinks and sang songs or gave speeches. She could see the discomfort in his face and heard it in his voice as he began to recite the lines.

The crowd fell silent, for his voice was passionate and clear, echoing in the quiet of the winter day. Captivating all who heard those words.

"*O fairest of the feather'd train! For whom I sing, for whom I* burn." He emphasized that word as his gaze held hers, and she realized in that moment that she was no longer breathing. "*Attend with pity to my strain. And grant my love a kind return.*"

Her heart was throbbing as he continued, recounting the courtship of the blackbirds to the enraptured crowd that was gathering closer with each word.

"*But trust me, love, the raven's wing. Is not to be compar'd with mine. Nor can the lark so sweetly sing. As I, who strength with sweetness join.*"

She was whispering the words out loud with him, her hands clenched before her, unable to tear her eyes away from him.

He looked so big standing on that bench. So broad and strong and in that moment he wasn't her friend. He was something else. And that terrified her and enraptured her all at once.

"He led her to the nuptial bower. And nestled closely to her side. The fondest bridegroom of that hour. And she the most delighted bride." His voice was rough now, strong but low and powerful.

And God help her, but a tremble worked through her body. He continued, but as he reached the last four stanzas, where the blackbirds flew into the wrong vale and encounter the gunner who would end their passions, he looked away.

That allowed the strange spell between them to break, and she staggered backward, turning from him as he finished the poem. Her hands shook as the party applauded, their sniffles indicating that all had been moved as she had once been by the tragic poem.

Only today, for the first time in many years, it hadn't been Andrew she thought of when those words were said. Today the poem had locked her with Cav. Linked her to him as much as the strangeness that had sprung up between them in these last few days.

She pivoted toward him and found he'd come down from the bench. The men were shaking his hand, the ladies all cooing and complimenting him.

"What a fine way to celebrate four colly birds, my lady!" Lord Weatherall said.

She forced a smile. "Indeed. It was kind of Mr. Cavendish to present one of my favorite poems for us this afternoon." She clapped her hands together trying to gather herself. "So I issue a challenge. Tonight after supper, when we reconvene in the parlor, I hope we will see many more presentations by you, my cherished guests. And the applause will be all the higher if you can incorporate colly birds of any kind in your recitation."

The crowd seemed excited by the idea, and groups of them moved off together toward the house, chattering about what they could present to outshine Cav's wonderful performance. She let out her breath in a shaky sigh. She needed to speak to him, of course. To thank him for how he had come to her rescue. To compliment him, as the others had, on his performance.

But he wasn't waiting for her. He was striding after the group, not looking back. His shoulders seemed tense, though. She knew that tension well after all these years. He was displeased, perhaps. With her?

She moved to follow, but one of the chaperones fell into pace beside her. Mrs. York, the American, mother to Bridget York. The woman had a wide smile as she said, "That truly was a lovely representation of the day's theme," she said. "This has been a creative and wonderful party. My daughter and I are so pleased to have been included."

Emily forced herself to be gracious and smiled at the woman. "And I am pleased to have you. I've spoken to Bridget a handful of times since her arrival, and you have much to be proud of."

Mrs. York's blush was Emily's reward, and normally she might have reveled in it or even pressed her companion to find out more about Bridget so she could better match her. But today she was still so distracted. Cav had entered the house now. Where would he go? With the crowd or off on his own?

"Mr. Cavendish is a wonderful orator," Mrs. York continued. "You and he are friends, I know."

Emily's lips suddenly felt dry and she shifted as they entered the house together. "Y-Yes. Mr. Cavendish was a great friend to my late husband and has remained just as faithful to me in the years since Andrew's death. He is the kindest and best of men."

"I have heard told he might be thinking of taking a bride when the Season begins in the spring. Would you know anything about that?"

Emily could scarcely hear anything with the blood rushing in her ears. She stared at Mrs. York, her hands trembling at her sides. Over the years, many a mama had sought out Cav for her quarry. A few had come to her and to Andrew, as Mrs. York was now, to obtain insider information about Cav.

But now the idea that he would seek a marriage felt more...raw... to Emily. Was it true? He was of an age, of course. She knew his grandfather believed it was past time for him to make his move and go forward into his destiny. But would Cav finally bow to the pressures at home?

"I-I do not know," she stammered, for she realized Mrs. York was still waiting for an answer. They had reached the parlor now, where some of the guests were gathered talking. It seemed some had retired to their chambers for an afternoon rest.

Cav was not amongst this group.

"Oh." Mrs. York looked slightly disappointed. "Well, I suppose all is fair, isn't it? Are you coming in with the others?"

Emily should have said yes, of course. A polite hostess would not allow her guests to linger on their own without her support. But right now she didn't give a damn about her duties. She could only think of Cav and this strange drive to get to him. To...see him after that display in the garden.

"I have a obligation to attend to, I'm afraid," she said. "But please, partake of refreshments and enjoy yourself. I will see you later in the day."

Mrs. York said something in return, but Emily hardly heard it. She hurried away, up the hall. Cav hadn't gone to bed, she didn't think. It wasn't his nature to rest his head after tea. No...she had a hunch he would go where he very often did when he visited Crossfox.

She was almost running now, racing through the winding halls until she found the room she was seeking. The light came from under the closed door, and she caught her breath before she opened it and entered the library.

He was there. Of course he was. He stood in the middle of the room and had stripped away his jacket, leaving him in a brocaded waistcoat, his shirtsleeves rolled to his elbows as he paced the room, not looking at the books on the shelves.

When she stepped into the room and shut the door behind herself, he stopped moving and just...stared at her. Just like in the garden the day before, just like in the same place less than a quarter hour earlier, that focused stare stole her breath. It made her feel like it was the first time he was looking at her, rather than the fiftieth, the hundredth, the thousandth time those dark blue eyes had held hers.

"Don't," he whispered.

She ignored the admonishment. If she listened to it, if she pulled away now, she might lose the closest friend she'd ever had. No, they just had to push past this. Pretend it away, didn't they? Act as though it had never happened and then it would disappear like smoke in the wind.

"Thank you," she said, wishing her voice didn't shake as she stepped toward him. His eyes came shut and he let out his breath in a long stream. "You saved me today."

"I would do so any day," he growled, his tone almost angry. "You know that."

She stopped moving, because he was as tightly wound as a spring. His jaw flexed, his hands fisted against his thighs, his mouth was a thin line with no hint of his usual playful smile.

"Cav," she said.

His eyes flew open. "Don't," he said again.

"Don't do what?" she asked.

"You know what," he retorted, scrubbing a hand through those curly locks, mussing them and making him all the more rakish and wicked looking. "You know what, even if you want to pretend you don't."

She was shaking so hard she thought she might fall over because in that moment the truth became painfully clear: Cav *wanted* her. He wanted her as he stood here in her library, holding himself back like he was trying to protect her from that feeling. From all the damage that feeling could do.

"We need to just pretend—" she started.

"Pretend," he repeated on a humorless laugh. "What do you think

I've been doing, Emily? What do you think every moment I'm in a room with you is?"

Her knees went weak and she staggered closer, even when she knew she should move further away. "You don't mean that. You can't *feel* that. You're my friend, aren't you?"

"Yes," he ground out. "I have always been your friend. I shall always be. But that doesn't mean there isn't more here, too. That I don't look at you and want to—"

He cut himself off with a curse that made her cheeks burn.

"We can ignore it," she suggested. "Ignore these desires."

His eyes went wide. "We," he repeated. "*We* can ignore it. What are *you* ignoring, Em?"

Her breath caught as she realized her slip. At what it had revealed to him. At what it revealed to her, too. It had been a long time since she felt...desire. And that was what this was. Desire. Hot and heavy, flowing from the deepest part of her. Something she feared she could not stop now that she recognized it, named it, claimed it even just in her own heart.

She desired Cav. What was worse was that the feeling didn't seem...new.

Her silence must have emboldened him because he eased a step closer to her this time. She looked up into his handsome face and no longer saw her friend. No, she saw something else, someone else, and when she leaned into him, it was because she couldn't do anything else.

He reached out a hand. It was shaking as he traced her jawline with a feather-light and gentle touch. A sigh escaping her lips because the pleasure of what he was doing was too, too much.

He leaned down and she lifted up, drawn to him like a magnet. Their lips were not a millimeter apart, and then not even that. Then he was kissing her and everything else faded away.

Cav brushed her mouth gently at first, just the stroke of his lips on hers. But as his hand closed around her bicep, the timidity of his kiss evaporated. The hesitation that was meant to give her an opportunity to escape. When she didn't take it, he took over and she felt every bit of his reputation as an experienced, passionate rake. He *claimed*. His mouth opened and she did the same. He dragged her against him with a rough groan and she clutched at his lapels for purchase as she tried to pull him even closer. His tongue speared past her lips, tasting her, exploring her, sucking her, teasing her. All she could do was surrender, softening beneath his touch as her entire body began to throb with a need she hadn't felt for years.

A need she recognized, despite the long separation from it. She wanted him to do more than kiss her. Right here in the library in the home she'd once shared with his best friend. With her husband.

And that thought tore through her mind and she yanked back.

"Cav," she whispered against his still-seeking lips. "Cav. *Cavendish!*"

He pulled away and took a long step back. His blue eyes were dilated to almost pure black, and his hands shook as he shoved them to his sides. They were silent for what felt like an eternity, each looking at the other, the weight of what they'd done hanging between them.

"I'm sorry," he finally said, "if I did something you didn't want."

She caught her breath. That was the worst part of all of this, in the end. It *was* something she wanted. She'd wanted him to kiss her, she'd taken enthusiastic part when he did. There was no lack of consent here. And that was wrong. But it felt so right.

"You shouldn't be sorry," she managed to croak out. "You did nothing wrong."

He arched a brow at her, as if challenging her to go further down that path. But she couldn't. Not right now when her head was spinning.

"I should—I should go," she gasped. "I shouldn't be here."

His shoulders rolled forward and his full lips, the ones she knew the feel of now, pursed and went white and flat. "As you wish. I would not keep you."

She paused, waiting for him to say something, anything. To make this right, just as he'd been making everything right for her for the last five years. But he didn't. He simply allowed for that kiss to hang between them.

Since she didn't know what to do with it, she staggered from the library, closing the door behind herself and leaning against it in the hall. She dragged great breaths into her lungs as she fought the strangest urge to just...cry. Tears of heartbreak, tears of confusion... tears of relief. She had kissed Cav and it was a *relief*, as if she'd been waiting for it for a long time.

"No, you're just confused," she said to herself as she marched to the stairs and upward. She needed to go to her room and calm herself. To touch herself, if need be, because everything felt hot and shaky, and perhaps *that* was why she was so confused about Cav. Whatever she planned to do, she needed to do it swiftly, before she ruined the closest friendship in her life.

Before she ruined everything.

∼

Cav stood, staring into the fire. Trying not to stare at the door where Emily had just departed. More to the point, trying not to follow her out that door, catch her arm and kiss her all over again.

Kiss her. Christ, he'd been dreaming of doing that for a decade. Haunting, aching dreams that made him hate himself and long for her all at once. He'd promised himself he would never betray Andrew, and he hadn't. But Andrew was dead now. Long dead, long gone. It was no less true just because it was heartbreaking.

Cav didn't owe the man allegiance anymore.

He sank into the chair before the fire and scrubbed a hand over his face. Emily's mouth had been so soft beneath his lips. She'd tasted faintly of tea and mint, of sweetness and passion. And when she'd gripped his lapels and lifted against him with that little sound of plea-sure that came from deep within her chest?

It made him hard just thinking about it. Thinking about that proof that she had wanted him in that heated, powerful moment as much as he wanted her. But was it permanent or fleeting? That was the question.

After Andrew's death, Cav had certainly considered what the future might hold. But her grief had been so powerful, so overwhelming, that he hadn't pursued his heart. Instead, he'd let their mutual love of Andrew bond them into deeper friends. In truth, he valued that friendship as much as he'd valued the one with her late husband.

Perhaps he valued it more. Emily didn't let many people near. She was friendly, of course, sunny and light and the kind of woman who would design an entire party over trying to help spinsters find true love. No one who met her could do anything but adore her.

But those friendships were surface, at best. She had lost so much, first Andrew, then her parents, in rapid succession that she had begun to hold others at arm's length. Except for Cav. She had let him in.

That had as much value as any kiss.

But damn, the kiss had been spectacular. Before she pushed him away. Before she ran from him, her face pale and streaked with fear and confusion.

"You knew it might be this way," he reminded himself as he got up and stirred the fire absently.

It was true. He hadn't ever assumed that if he showed his hand to her, let her see his desire...or his love...that she would automatically accept it. She would need to think on it. She might even run from it.

But now it was out. At least on some level. And he would just have to wait and see how she would respond next. He'd been patient this long. Staying the course was the best way to end this game of chess. He only hoped he would end up with the queen.

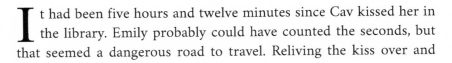

It had been five hours and twelve minutes since Cav kissed her in the library. Emily probably could have counted the seconds, but that seemed a dangerous road to travel. Reliving the kiss over and over to the distraction of all other conversation or activity was dangerous enough.

Even at supper, she hadn't been able to take her eyes off of him, down on the opposite end of the table, talking and smiling with other guests. Comfortable, as if kissing her hadn't meant anything to him.

Perhaps it...didn't? Despite how kind Cav always was to her, how perfectly proper when they were together, his game of catch and release with women was well known. He took lovers—he wasn't particularly secretive about it. But he never courted anyone. So perhaps kissing her was some continuation of that game he played.

That sat in her chest like a rock. The party had moved to the parlor and everyone was talking and laughing as they prepared for the presentations they'd planned earlier. Cav stood at the window, leaning against the wall beside it, arms folded as he watched the scene play out. His gaze darted to her, and her heart throbbed.

The reaction became even stronger when he pushed from the wall and made his slow way across the room to her. There was a fluidity in his movements, a certainty she had never marked before. A swagger that announced to the room that he was a man who knew what a lady needed. She'd never felt that directed toward her, but there it was, aimed firmly at her. She shivered as he stopped a foot away.

"Lady Rutledge," he said, loud enough that the room could hear.

She couldn't speak. She couldn't breathe. She fought to do both. "Yes, Mr. Cavendish?"

"Perhaps you'd like to begin the presentations," he suggested, his tone gentle. Her friend back, rather than the man who had held her so close and kissed her so thoroughly.

She shook her head and felt heat creep into her cheeks. "Of course. Yes."

She moved past him and to the fire where the chairs in the room had all been turned. Somehow she managed to keep a smile on her face as she reminded the party that anyone could exhibit and how including colly birds of any variety, from crow to raven to blackbird, would inspire more applause.

The party was jolly and immediately many raised their hand to participate. Emily came back to her spot to watch from afar, but she could scarcely find pleasure in the exercise, no matter how much laughter and light filled that happy room.

Because Cav had returned to his spot by the window. And though he occasionally glanced at her, he made no move to join her. To touch her. To connect with her again. So she was left wondering if the kiss that had meant so much to her meant anything to him.

And why it stung so much that something that never should have happened was so unimportant to Cav.

CHAPTER 6

FIVE GOLD RINGS

I t was probably too cold for what Emily had in mind on the fifth day of the party. But there were so few options for the five gold rings in the Christmas poem that she felt backed into a corner.

Actually, backed into a corner was what she felt in general at present. All night she'd thought of Cav and the weight of his mouth on hers, the taste of him, the slide of his tongue that promised so much more. And yet he'd avoided her. He'd been avoiding her all of this day, as well. Even now he stood as far away from her as he could, on the opposite side of the group. His arms were folded across that broad chest as he spoke to Lady Abigail and never looked in Emily's direction.

Emily was beginning to get frustrated by it all.

"You are so creative, my lady," came a voice to her right.

Emily jumped, for she hadn't realized that Lady Mulberry had joined her. "I—thank you, my lady," she responded with difficulty. She scanned the gathering group of partygoers and frowned. "I do not see your daughters in the crowd."

The viscountess shifted and her discomfort was clear. "They are... sensitive to the cold, my lady, and have cried off the festivities with their sincere apologies."

Emily worried her lip. She had been looking for a distraction from thoughts of Cav's kiss, but this was not something more pleasant. She had plans, after all, and this put a damper on them.

"Oh," she said slowly. "Well...that is a shame. I do understand, though. We have been lucky that the weather has been mild during this party, but today there is a nip to the air that goes a bit deeper." She frowned and gathered her woolen pelisse closer. "I hope the others are not equally upset by the choice of activity. We will be moving and that should help."

"I'm sure they won't be," Lady Mulberry reassured her, but didn't look as certain as she sounded as she patted Emily's hand and then slipped back to the crowd.

Emily barely resisted the urge to huff out a breath in frustration. Oh, why did everything have to be so complicated? These endeavors had seemed so perfect in her mind. She would pair off everyone and Cav would help her. But no one was cooperating in their pairings, and Cav had kissed her and then walked away.

She shook her head. No. She would not get wrapped up in the bad. She would focus on her next step.

"I realize it is cold, but the fifth day of Christmas presents us with gold rings." She nodded, and footmen appeared from the house with large hoops. "And while these are only painted gold, I think you will find them to be an exhilarating way to pass the time. We are going to the top of the hill yonder—" She pointed off in the close distance to a rise. "And racing the hoops down."

There was a burst of laughter at the idea of all these adults participating in a child's game, but no one argued. "I have paired you off again for the race. You must stay together as you guide your hoop down to the finish line. In fact, you will be required to link arms as you do so."

There was an excited murmur at that scandalous suggestion, which was exactly what Emily had wanted. In the country she could get away with such a thing, couldn't she?

She announced the pairs, linking the ladies with either gentlemen they hadn't been exposed to yet or ones she thought might have made a connection of some kind. Then she frowned. She had expected to pair the twins with two of the male guests, but now she would have to pair chaperones instead. Though she supposed that could still lead to the match for one of the younger ladies in attendance. The chaperones would work on the gentlemen, as they always did.

"And since the Ladies Honoria and Prudence are not joining us this afternoon, I will ask that Lady Mulberry pair with Lord Levenridge." She glanced over the crowd and smiled at Abigail Delafield's paid companion, Miss Hester Bright. "And Miss Bright will pair with Mr. Powell."

"And who will *you* partner with, Lady Rutledge?" Lord Weatherall asked as he offered his arm to Lady Thea, who he had been paired with.

Emily caught her breath. She had been so busy making the pairings for everyone else, she hadn't thought about who *she* would take as a partner in the race. Well...that wasn't entirely true. She had always known she would pair with Cav. After all, she wasn't matching him at this event and she could depend on him.

But that was weeks ago. And now things were different. But who else was available? She had paired all the gentlemen and ladies and chaperones. If she changed anything now, it would make the odd rift between her and Cav a matter of public record. Not something she wanted for the rumor mill, nor for the future of their friendship.

"With Mr. Cavendish, of course. I always give myself the best advantage when it comes to a friendly competition."

Cav smiled slightly as the crowd laughed and took the last hoop from the footman before he crossed the lawn to her. He offered an arm to her as he glanced down. "My lady."

Oh, that was right. She had insisted the pairs join arms. So she couldn't avoid touching him. Something she'd done so often, but never after being kissed thoroughly in the library. Now she stared at that strong arm, muscles plain even beneath the layers of greatcoat.

She wanted so much to touch him. Too much. When she did, folding her fingers at the crook of his elbow, it was like someone sucked the air from her lungs. Her head spun and she curled her toes in her warm boots.

"To the hill," she croaked out, pointing off in the distance. The others headed off, with her and Cav in the rear. Without all the eyes in the party on them she felt more comfortable in examining his face, trying to read what he thought or felt today.

It was impossible. His expression was impassive aside from his tightly pressed lips. Lips she knew the feel of. Damn it, she had to stop thinking about that.

But still, he didn't speak as the couples lined up at the top of the hill. She forced herself to focus on the plan and said, "Ready, set...go!"

When she said the last, the couples launched, hustling down the hill as they tried to push their hoops in any semblance of control. She and Cav did the same. He pushed the hoop and they followed, taking turns tapping it to try to keep it in line. It should have been fun. Under any other circumstance it would have been. Cav was always up for a game, he never put ego above enjoyment. And yet neither of them was laughing.

She hated it. Hated that the moment in the library had changed things. She didn't *want* things to change. She wanted to depend on this man as her friend forever. Except now she also wanted more. Like a fool.

Her distraction had consequences, just as everything in life did. When Cav tapped the hoop toward her, she didn't catch it soon enough to tap it in a straight line, and it careened off toward the opposite side of the hill, where it bounced out of sight.

She released Cav and they raced after it together, out of sight of the rest of the party, who were all laughing and stumbling toward the bottom of the hill and the makeshift finish line her staff had created with a long line of bright Christmas ribbon.

"There it is!" she said, and pointed to the hoop, which had come to rest near a little pile of rocks amongst the dead grass and long faded wildflowers.

Cav grunted but didn't speak as they reached it together. She picked it up with one hand and then faced him. "Cav, please won't you talk to me?"

She realized as she spoke that she was worrying her gold wedding ring, the one she still wore, and Cav's face grew stormy as he turned away from her with a snort.

"What is the point in speaking when I know your face better than any other? I can see what you're going to say without hearing it," he said. "You're going to recite an entire soliloquy about how we shouldn't have done what we did in the library, aren't you?"

She froze. That *had* been her intention, after all. To tell Cav that they couldn't repeat the imprudence of the kiss. But now, staring at him, his face fierce in the cold, his eyes holding hers and flashing with emotion and something...hotter...bolder...she didn't *want* to say that.

He shook his head when she didn't respond, and pivoted as if to walk away. She didn't know how she moved or how she came up with the imprudent plan that followed. But she gasped and leapt forward, gliding the hoop over his head so that he couldn't go forward.

He spun around in the circle and arched a brow at her. "Fine. If you want to do this, I suppose there has never been any stopping you. Do you have something to say, Emily?"

"You're right. I-I don't want to ruin our friendship," she whispered, and wished she could say it more strongly. But it all felt so charged now. So dangerous.

"We don't have to ruin our friendship," he huffed out.

She shook her head and tugged on the hoop, forcing him closer a step. She stared up into his dark eyes and fought the shiver that wracked her from head to toe.

"How could we not?" she whispered. "I...*want* you and it's...it is bound to turn everything on its head."

His eyes went wide and his hand fluttered at his side, as if he wished to touch her. "You—you want me?" he repeated, shock heavy on every word.

She nodded. She knew she shouldn't nod. Knew she shouldn't uncork this bottle, because she would never be able to close it again. It would never be the same. But neither would it be the same if she felt this ache, this horrible, powerful, wonderful thing…and never let it out.

"Lady Rutledge! Mr. Cavendish!"

The voices were coming from the other side of the hill and she dropped the hoop in surprise. Cav stepped away as a few of the guests crested the hill and descended upon them.

Emily forced herself to laugh up at them. "We went off course, I'm afraid, and only just managed to get our hoop under control."

Cav bent, took the hoop and waggled it toward the others. "We'll come around to the other side of the hill now. I cannot wait to hear who won the day." He sounded so normal, but as the others strode back toward the finish line, he glanced down at her.

"We can't talk about this here and now," she said.

He arched a brow. "No. But we aren't finished talking about it either."

She caught her breath. She'd seen Cav turn that heated stare on a few ladies over the years. Normally when he didn't know she was looking. But now it was focused on her and it was transformative. She was no longer any of the things which had defined her for so long. She didn't feel like a widow or a lady or a friend.

She felt something else. She felt like a lover, waiting for that first caress. She felt like an instrument ready to be played.

"No, we aren't," she managed to choke out. "Will you…" She trailed off because the suggestion she wanted to make was a point of no return.

"Will I what?" he pressed.

She swallowed past the lump in her throat and croaked out, "Will you come talk to me in my private parlor after we return from the gathering and the others go to rest or entertain themselves before supper?"

His eyes widened a fraction, but then the flash of heat she'd noted earlier flared even higher. An inferno contained by a sea of blue, and she shivered because her body knew what that inferno would do if she let it. What he wanted to do, despite a history of friendship.

"Yes, my lady," he said. Then he offered her his arm and guided her off toward the others.

They didn't speak of it again as they walked around the hill to where the others were gathered, laughing and partaking in wassail. But what they had agreed to hung between them. And that was terrifying and thrilling and like nothing she had ever experienced before in her life.

~

Cav felt like he was coming out of his skin as he and the rest of the party came into the warmth of the parlor an hour later. Of course, he'd felt that way since kissing Emily the previous night.

But now she'd asked him to join her in her private parlor, and that meant...everything. Or at least, it could mean everything. If she let it. If he did.

"Supper will be at seven," Emily said, smiling at the crowd with the same brightness as she always did. No one would think she was carrying some kind of wicked plan. "And I hope you will enjoy yourselves until then."

The party separated with that permission. A few of the gentlemen started off down the hall. Lord Allington was one of them, and he pivoted back toward Cav. "We were going to play a round of billiards, Cavendish. Care to join?"

"No, I think I'll rest a bit," he said.

Allington wrinkled his brow as if confused by that suggestion, but then he shrugged and off they went.

"I think that is a fine idea, Mr. Cavendish," Emily said. "A party like this one is bound to wear out the mind."

He arched a brow and leaned closer, whispering, "Laying it on a bit thick, aren't you?"

She glared at him and he smiled. At least they hadn't entirely lost their ability to banter. No matter what came out of this party and whatever was about to happen, he didn't want that. That was what had kept him from pursuing her. He'd rather long for her than lose her because he had pushed too far.

And yet here they were. She bid her farewells to the group and started up the stairs with just a backward glance toward him. He waited a few moments, chatting with Lady Hickson and Lady Mulberry for a brief moment before he excused himself and went up the stairs himself.

He glanced down to make sure no one was watching, and when it was clear he was safe to do so, went right instead of left into the family wing of bedchambers. He counted the doors, just as he'd done a dozen times over the years when he'd come here. Counting his way to her, but never doing anything about it when he got to her chamber.

Today he lifted his hand and hesitated. Emily had claimed she didn't want to destroy their friendship, and he had insisted they didn't have to do that. But he knew that was a lie. Just a kiss had changed things between them. Anything more and...well, he wouldn't think of it.

He knocked, and there was a flutter of movement from within before Emily opened the door. She ducked her head out, checking in the hall before she motioned him in.

"I was careful, I assure you," he said, noting how pale her cheeks were and how she worried her hands before her after she closed the door behind him.

He took a step away from her and looked around the private parlor. He'd never been in this room, and he smiled because it looked so much like her. He smiled because it looked nothing like Andrew, and that made all of this much easier.

"A pretty view," he said as he moved to the window and looked down over the garden. In the distance he could see the lake, and judging by how the birds were waddling on its surface, it was frozen by the cold.

"Y-yes," she said softly. "I have always loved that view. I'll miss it when this room is no longer mine."

He turned toward her. "No longer yours?"

She shrugged. "Andrew has been gone a long time, and his family has indulged me by allowing me to still call this home my own. But I know you've heard that his younger brother has found a bride. Once they are married, it would be wrong of me to continue to pretend I am Lady Rutledge and that this home is mine. I need to...to move on."

He frowned. He happened to agree with that assessment, for his own not entirely selfless reasons. But he didn't want her to use whatever was happening between them as some unwanted push toward her next chapter.

"Emily," he said softly.

She took a long step toward him. "I-I don't know what to do, Cav," she said. "I've always known what to do, especially when it came to you and me. I've always known what we were. But now it's all...different."

He nodded as he moved toward her, closing the distance between them until he could touch her hand if he reached out. He didn't yet. Emily had always been the sort who needed to talk things out. He wasn't about to rush her past that.

"You know better than most that things can't stay the same," he said. "In the end, we're always going to have to move."

"But toward what?" she whispered. "I've put off deciding that so long and now it's here. And everything is suddenly so confusing. And then you kissed me—"

He held his breath as she looked at him, her gaze fluttering over his lips like she was reliving that kiss.

"—you kissed me and my head is spinning and I don't know what to embrace or fear now. I just know that nothing can be the same again. And I'm afraid of that and I'm thrilled by that and—"

He did reach for her then, and tugged her against him. She broke off her sentence, her breath going short as he cupped her chin and tilted it up toward him. The last time he'd kissed her, he hadn't planned for it. It was a volcano after years of pressure building up beneath the surface.

This time, though, he savored it. He lived for the catch of her breath, for the way her lips parted slightly just as he brushed his mouth over hers. He drowned in how she opened to him, allowing him in as her arms came around his neck. She tasted like honey, so sweet it was almost overpowering, and he lost all sense of reason when she lifted against him with a soft, guttural moan of pleasure.

She wanted him. Not just when she was swept away by a moment, but she'd admitted she felt the same even when her feet were firmly on the ground. He had pined for her, ached for her, burned for her for so long. How could he resist if there were any option at all that he could have even a taste of heaven?

Just a taste would be enough, wouldn't it?

She tensed in his arms and he drew back, looking down at her without releasing her. She looked so conflicted, so lost, and he shook his head. "I can stop."

"I don't want you to stop," she admitted, and her cheeks went pink. "I just don't know how to say what I *do* want. Not to you."

He slid his hands down her back, memorizing the feel of every curve of her body. She shivered as she lifted against him.

"You want this," he whispered, and cupped her backside. Her eyes went wide, but she didn't pull away. Instead she nodded. He ground her against him, letting her feel the hardness of him as it grazed her softness. "You want this."

This time her response was a garbled hiss. "Yes."

"You want this." He ducked his head and kissed her again, and she dug her fingers into his hair, fingers abrading his scalp as she tilted her head and deepened the kiss with wild desperation.

He quivered with the desire that had pulsed through him for so many years he almost couldn't remember a time when it didn't exist. And now it was about to be brought to fruition because he was going to make love to this woman. To Emily. He was going to make love to her until she quaked beneath his touch.

And if he was lucky enough or skillful enough or strong enough, perhaps that would open the door to something more. The thing he dared not name as she whispered his name into his mouth. For now this was enough and he wouldn't let go.

CHAPTER 7

C av was unbuttoning her dress. Emily was vaguely aware of it as she kissed him and kissed him while the world outside the door faded away. He was unbuttoning her dress with those strong, lean fingers that obviously knew what they were doing. It was in that moment that she fully grasped what would happen between them.

She could stop it. If she said no, he would pull away. If she demanded he never touch her like this again, he would obey.

But she didn't want that. She wanted this wicked, wonderful stolen moment so much that she could hardly stay upright. Luckily strong hands supported her, just as they had supported her for years.

She trusted him. That mattered more than anything.

He broke his mouth from hers, his breath coming in desperate pants as he glided her dress away from her shoulders, down her arms, past her breasts, her waist, and let it crumple on the ground between them. He stared at her in her chemise, the thin straps and soft fabric barely covering her curves. He licked his lips and her body twitched in response.

"Before you…before you take off the rest," she gasped, feeling the burning heat of her cheeks. She must look like a plum!

He nodded and dropped his hands, clenching them in fists at his sides as if he were forced to do that to maintain control. "Yes?"

"Aside from my maid, no one has seen me like this in years," she whispered. "I don't know if I'll please you. I don't know if I know how to please anyone anymore and I'm...I'm..."

"Nervous?" he asked softly, his deep voice soothing as much as it was stimulating. How could it be both?

"Yes," she admitted, and bent her head.

He tucked a finger beneath her chin and forced her to look up at him again. His gaze focused on hers, held her steady, centered her as she had come to depend on him to do. He smiled, something slow and heated.

"There is no way you won't please me, Emily, I promise you that," he whispered. "And I know it's been a long time for you. All you have to do is just...trust me. And let me take care of you."

Tears stung her eyes at those words. She reached up and traced his jawline with her palm, and he leaned into it with a shudder. "You have always taken care of me," she murmured.

He nodded, the faint stubble rubbing her palm.

She stepped back and drew in a long breath, then pulled the straps of her chemise down and let it fall to the floor beside the dress. She was revealed, and she felt every inch of her skin as he gazed down over her.

"Christ," he muttered, then leaned in and caught her cheeks, kissing her again.

This time there was desperation in his touch, hunger that she responded to with her own as he backed her toward the settee by the fire. He settled her onto it gently and then stepped away to shed his jacket, unwind his cravat and tug his shirt over his head.

She pushed up on her elbows and dazzled at what he revealed. Cav and Andrew couldn't have been two more different men in appearance. Andrew had been thick and strong and built to carry a broadsword in wars of old. Cav would have been a general. He had a leaner strength, a finer build but no less compelling with his defined shoulders and tapered waist. His stomach muscles bunched as he dropped to his knees before the settee.

He smiled up at her as he loosened her bootstrap and pulled first one, then the other off, followed by her stockings. When he tossed them away, she was truly, fully naked, and she found herself settling her legs open a fraction. A delicate invitation for what was to come.

The reality of that was still shocking, but she wanted it more, not less.

"You are so beautiful," he whispered, she thought almost more to himself than to her. Her eyes stung with those words anyway. It had been a long time since a man had whispered such a thing when she was wanton and vulnerable before him. She hadn't realized how much she missed it until that very moment.

His fingers traced delicate patterns along her calves, trails that swooped higher and higher. When he cupped the back of her knee, she let out a hiss of pleasure that made his pupils dilate further. He pressed a palm against the inside of each of her thighs and widened her legs, opening her to him in a more intimate way.

She turned her head into her shoulder as he stared at her, wondering what he thought. Wondering what he would do next. He pressed his thumbs to her outer lips and she ground against him out of instinct. Then he peeled her open.

The warm breeze of the fire brushed her sensitive sex, but it was swiftly replaced by the heat of his breath. She glanced down, mesmerized as he lowered his mouth and licked her.

She dug her fingers into his hair, lifting to his tongue as he swept it across her again. He watched her as he licked, and she gave him a show because she couldn't do anything but. The sensation was too powerful for her to mince or pretend it didn't move her. After so long, after receiving pleasure only from her hand, what he was doing with his lips and his tongue was overpowering.

He took his time, tasting and teasing, massaging her inner thighs as he delved her deeper into the madness of building pleasure. And just when she felt like she would be lost on these building waves forever, he pressed a finger to her entrance.

She froze, lifting up on her elbows to watch as he glided that finger inside. She flexed against him with a low moan, her back arching and her fingers clenching hard against the cushions as he slowly began to thrust into her body. He returned his mouth to her sex, but this time he was more focused. He no longer teased but put all his attention on her clitoris.

And when he began to suck gently, repeatedly, consistently, the pleasure that had been slowly meandering through her seemed to hit a tipping point. She ground hard against his finger and he added a second one, letting her long-neglected body adjust to the invasion even as he tongued and sucked her to the brink.

She was going to fall. She knew it. She reveled in that brief moment when the sensation crested, and then she tumbled into pleasure. Wave after wave of it washed over her. She shook and slapped a hand over her mouth so her keening cries wouldn't alert the entire household to what was happening here in her parlor.

He dragged her through the crisis, pulling more and more pleasure from her until she flopped, weak and spent, against the settee cushions. He kissed her thigh and she shivered, watching through a hooded gaze as he glided his mouth across her hip, along her stomach, between her breasts. How he could wake desire in her again so swiftly, she didn't know, but by the time he took her mouth she was aching again.

She tasted herself on his lips, his tongue, and wound her arms around his bare shoulders as she drank of her own pleasure. When he pulled away, she stared up at him, so close and so warm and so...hers in this moment that couldn't last.

"I hope I served you well, my lady," he said with a crooked grin.

She laughed despite the emotions bubbling deep in her chest. "Very well. Did the keening not make it obvious?"

"The keening was a fine indication." His gaze slid over her face.

"I'm going to ask you a question, and I want you to have the understanding that there is no wrong answer."

Her heart thudded at the seriousness with which he observed her. "What is it?"

"Would you like me to...continue?" he asked, sliding a hand up her side, letting his thumb caress the underside of her breast in a most distracting fashion. "Or stop?"

She stared at him. There had been no thought in her mind that he would pleasure her and then leave without taking his own relief. There had been no assumption that he wouldn't take her the moment he started touching her.

His expression was impassive but for the heat in his eyes, and she almost shook her head in wonder. But of course he would offer her this. Cav had been taking care of her for years, sometimes at his own detriment, she knew. It was his nature, perhaps, to make sure those he cared for were safe and comforted.

She traced his cheek with her fingers and smiled up at him. "If you stop now I will make sure the entertainment for tomorrow is six geese hissing at you, not a-laying."

"Thank God," he groaned, resting his forehead against her shoulder with a laugh. "I'm hard as steel—I would not have survived the walk back to my chamber."

She might have laughed at the image of him limping to his chamber, but the idea that he was hard as steel was too fascinating. She pushed at his shoulders to make him lean away.

"Show me," she whispered.

His eyes went wide and the laughter left his face. His expression went hard and hot and heavy. In that moment, he looked every inch the rogue, the rake, the man of his reputation, but not any action he'd ever brought to her doorstep. She shivered at this part of him that was a stranger to her. This part that would bring her to shattering pleasure all over again, that was clear by his expression.

He shoved to his feet and stared down at her for a long moment. Then he moved to the chair across from the settee. He removed his boots and unfastened the fall front of his trousers. When he stood, it dropped away, and she caught her breath.

It had been a very long time since she saw a man unclothed, let alone a man at attention for her. She'd forgotten how compelling a hard cock was. She crooked her finger to bring him closer. When he was within arm's length, she reached for him, tracing just a fingertip along the hardness of him.

It was impossible not to compare him to Andrew, and she hated herself for thinking of her husband when she was about to bed another. But Andrew was her point of reference, her only lover until tonight. Cav was thicker, if Andrew had been longer, and as she closed her hand around his girth, she let out an involuntary sigh. God, she wanted this, wanted *him* deep inside of her. She stroked him and he staggered slightly as his fingers came down to dig into her hair. Pins pulled free as he clenched her hair, tilting her face up to look at him while she fisted him.

"Get up," he said, soft but firm. "Please."

She laughed at the added *please*, because this was an order. One she wished to follow. She released him and got to her feet, trembling with certainty of what she desired, but uncertainty at what would actually happen now.

He pushed his trousers away before he caught her in his arms, dragging her flush with his bare chest as he kissed her. Skin touched skin, so much skin, and she let out a little groan at how delicious the slide was. Her hands began to rove, smoothing over his back, his sides, his chest as he kissed her. She felt a wild desire to memorize his body, so she could recreate this in her dreams and fantasies. There would certainly be many of those once this stolen moment ended.

Perhaps she should have felt guilty about that truth, but she didn't. Not yet, anyway.

As she touched him, he was doing the same. His rough palm slid beneath one breast, lifting it as he stroked his thumb over her nipple. She broke from the kiss with a gasp and dipped her head back as pleasure ricocheted through her.

"You are magical," she murmured.

He chuckled. "Not quite."

She would beg to differ, but words were so hard to find as their bodies moved against each other, their hands explored with increasing urgency. The hardness of his cock pressed firmly into her belly, and she pushed against it, desperate for that moment when she would have more of him. All of him.

That seemed to tip the scales. He cursed beneath his breath and then pulled her back toward the settee. Only this time he didn't rest her against the pillows—instead he took a seat, sprawling out as he tugged her down to his lap. He cocked her leg over his and she straddled him, her sex stroking his cock as she ground down hopelessly.

"I would love to take a lifetime to just pleasure you and ready you," he said, his breathing sharp. "But I'm so bloody out of control, Emily, and our time is so short."

She nodded, for she felt the same way. She caught him, stroking his length once more before she aligned his body with hers. When she wiggled down, he entered her an inch, and she gasped with a pleasure-pain combination.

"It hurts?" he asked, his brow furrowing with concern the way it sometimes did.

Seeing that familiar expression centered her in this wild moment, and she nodded. "It's just been a very long time."

"We'll go slowly," he assured her as he caught her hips and pulsed up gently, claiming the next inch. "Even though it may kill me."

She laughed at his strangled voice and his focused expression. The ripple of her giggle made her grip him harder, and both of them caught their breath together. He surged up again, taking a little more.

The stretching pain had faded now, replaced by slick, welcoming pleasure. She squeezed his length with her inner muscles, reveling at this familiar, long-missed sensation of a man's body joined with hers.

This man's body. He was not a replacement. He was specifically what she wanted more than anything else in the world in that moment. When he fully seated himself deep inside of her, she jolted with renewed pleasure.

He held still, though, not thrusting, not encouraging her to do the same. He massaged her backside as he caught one breast and latched his mouth around her already hard nipple.

"Oh God," she gasped, clutching him closer as she began to grind down. She couldn't resist. She needed what he could provide. She would take it.

He met her strokes, lifting his hips as she lowered her own and they fell into a natural, gentle rhythm that built her pleasure back up to even higher heights than she had experienced with his mouth. She lost herself in it, riding him, focusing in turn on each part of her that sang beneath his touch.

This time when she came he had to catch her cries with his mouth, sucking hard on her tongue as she rode him out of control. His fingers pressed hard into her hips, hard enough to bruise, and she didn't care. She wanted those marks that would remind her this had been real when it felt like a dream later.

Only when she drooped against him, weak from release, did he carefully shift her onto her back on the pillows. He pulled from her kiss, watching her face as he increased the pace of his strokes. She stared, mesmerized by his focus, by the way his jaw tightened and his shoulders shook as he took what he needed. Took what only she could provide. He let out a gasping cry in the quiet and pulled from her body. She caught his spurting cock, stroking him through the pleasure as he writhed above her.

Then he collapsed down, his breath hot on her neck. His hands shaking as he smoothed them over her sweat-dampened skin. It was quiet for a long time before he lifted his head.

"Are you...well?" he asked.

She stared at him. Even in this moment, he wanted to take care of her, just as he always took care of her. How lucky she was to have a person like him in her life. And how lost she would be if he weren't there anymore.

That thought sobered her, but she managed to keep a smile on her face. "I am very well, Cav," she whispered. "I promise you."

That seemed to appease him, for he lifted himself off of her and got up. He began searching out their tangled clothing, handing over item by item to her first. He helped her smooth and button, putting her back together. Only when she moved to her mirror to tend to her hair did he put his own clothing back on. She watched him in the reflection as he fixed himself. Wished in that unguarded moment that she could just keep him undone and wild in her bed. That she could forget the world outside for a little longer. Perhaps never let it and all its uncertainty back in.

But she couldn't. This had been a moment. The moment had passed. What would happen next...well, she couldn't lose him as a friend. That was all that mattered now.

She smiled as she faced him. "Do I look presentable?"

His gaze flickered over her and he shifted. "Always," he said, his voice low and rough.

She started as she realized that was desire in his tone. And that she'd heard that same thing from him many times over the years. But that wasn't possible. She pushed it aside.

"They'll begin gathering for pre-supper drinks in an hour," she said, glancing at the clock on the mantel and wondering at how the time had flown while he pleasured her.

"Yes," he said softly. "And you will need to ready yourself. As will I. So I'll go." He took her hand and squeezed it, then moved to the door. There he stopped and looked back at her. "I hope you will never have occasion to regret this, Emily."

She shook her head. "I never will."

She said it with strength and it appeased him, for he smiled before he stepped out of her chamber. When he was gone, though, the uncertainty took over. Everything in her life was about to change. She'd known that before she came to the country, before she concocted this wild idea for a party. Cav was her constant...though she hoped what she said was true. She hoped she'd never regret this surrender, and she also knew she would if it meant things with him would change.

He was all she had, in the end. She couldn't lose him for something so foolish as desire. She wouldn't.

~

Cav sat at the end of the long table, far from Emily's side, and watched her. She was observing the room, and he could see that she was...troubled.

The worry was partly because of him. He knew that. When she looked at him, she blushed every time. She worried her hands before her. She fidgeted as she was sometimes wont to do because she was nervous or uncertain.

He'd wanted her forever, and having her had been more powerful, more wonderful, more satisfying than he'd pictured in even his most heated and hedonistic dreams. Even now as he imagined the squeeze of her sex around his, the soft surrender of her gasps of pleasure, his body reacted.

He knew she'd been happy while they were in each other's arms. But now she was thinking. Always thinking. One of her best qualities, until it spiraled her into a dozen worst-case futures. He could see her doing that now when she looked at him. See her writing a tale where their friendship ended because she'd let him lick her until she cried out his name in the quiet.

"Bollocks," he grunted beneath his breath. He was going to have to tread lightly now. Be careful in how he approached her while she stewed.

He couldn't lose her. He wouldn't.

He took a sip of wine and watched as her gaze flitted over the table. If she was troubled when she looked at him, she was equally so as she surveyed her matchmaking kingdom. In the last five days, he'd watched her move her pieces around the chessboard, placing ladies with gentlemen, forcing them into positions where they would talk or play together. But her matchmaking was failing.

Tonight the table was listless. Conversations were subdued if they happened at all. The gentlemen talked to each other, the ladies amongst themselves and with their chaperones.

Emily's experiment seemed to be a failure. And from the frown on her face, that troubled her deeply. She had always been the type to think of something wild and wonderful and play it out. She'd taken to new hobbies easily and enjoyed all types of pastimes. Sometimes they didn't work, but she'd also taken her losses with a laugh. She'd always been able to see them as a way to learn, rather than something darker or more desperate.

But this...this was different. She looked truly troubled by the fact her matchmaking wasn't going as planned. Her nostrils flared slightly, her hands shook as she lifted her wineglass to her lips, she was distracted when a servant came to take her plate.

Why, he couldn't understand. But he needed to. He needed to reach out and offer her the help and comfort she had asked him here to provide. The friendship he'd been providing for a decade.

But not tonight. Tonight she was too fraught when she looked at him. It was best to leave her be. Let her settle and see that he wouldn't push her into something she needed more time to allow.

But tomorrow, he was going to talk to her. About the party. About them. About everything.

CHAPTER 8

SIX GEESE A-LAYING

The next morning dawned cold and crisp, and Cav could see his breath as he swung down from his horse, Hank, patting the animal's flank gently. Once again he'd been unable to sleep, and this time he'd risen early for a ride through the estate on this, the last day of the year.

Crossfox was beautiful, with rolling hills, a small lake and enough woods to lose oneself in. Close enough to London to make the half-day's journey easy, but far enough out that it was quiet. Peaceful.

How many wonderful times had he shared with Andrew here? And later with Andrew and Emily. They'd always included him in their fun. Of course, Andrew had never suspected Cav's feelings for his wife. He had to assume that would have altered their friendship. Ended it.

He looked up on the hill. What was up there...*that* was really why he'd taken his ride out here this morning, no matter what other excuses he'd made about wanting to exercise his horse or needing the bracing enjoyment of a ride to clear his head.

No, he hadn't come for those things. He'd come for this.

He climbed up the rise to the flat on top and caught his breath. This was the family plot, where the Rutledge line had planted their dead for decades, centuries even. He moved through the lines of well-tended headstones until he came to the most recent of their ranks.

"*Andrew Rutledge, Tenth Viscount. Husband, Son, Friend,*" he read out loud, and his stomach ached with every word.

Five years his friend had been in this hallowed ground, and sometimes it still felt like yesterday. The hole left in his heart was not one that would ever truly be filled. He'd accepted that a long time ago.

"I did something," he said to the stone. His voice was shaky, as if he were admitting this to his friend in life, not death. "I knew you better than anyone, and you me, but I have no idea if you would accept it or rise from that grave to punch me in the face."

The only sound was the distant rustle of leaves in the brisk breeze. "I hope you would consent."

He shook his head and looked down toward the manor house in the distance. He found Emily's window because he knew exactly which one it was, even from so far away. He let out his breath in a ragged sigh.

"I never made a move while you lived, you know. I loved her as you loved her, and I never would have said a thing. I would have watched you two be happy together until the end of time, and I would have smiled about it because you both deserved the devotion you found in each other."

He rested a hand on the curve of the stone and clenched his fingers as intense grief washed through him. "But you're *not* here now, mate. It's the worst thing in the world, the greatest pain of my life and of hers, but it's true. I love her and I know this is my last chance to have a future with her. So I have to take it. I *need* to take it. But I wanted to tell you...man to man."

He shook his head. "Friend to friend. I just wish I could know if you approved it."

As he said the last, there was a great rush of sound behind him. He turned to watch as at least twenty pheasants rose from the heavy brush in the wooded area below the burial plot. Nothing that he could see would have spooked them, and his heart ached as he glanced back at Andrew's grave.

They had hunted pheasant on this property dozens of times over the years. It was one of their favorite pastimes when they came here. He smiled.

"I will take that as a yes," he said with a chuckle. "And I'd best take that yes and go back before you send me some other sign and confuse me." He rested his hand on the gravestone again. "You cannot fully grasp how much you are missed, my dearest friend. You cannot understand how deeply you are still loved."

Tears stung his eyes, and he blinked them away as he headed back down the hill and gathered up his horse. He took one last glance up the hill and then swung up and headed back toward the estate house, his mind telling him a hundred tales of good times with his old friend.

He was still lost in memory as he rode into the stable and dismounted, handing off the reins to a stable hand. The young man looked a bit flustered as he took the horse, glancing off behind him every few seconds.

"What is it?" Cav asked, confused by the young man's distraction.

Before the boy could answer, Cav heard the sound. A loud squawking followed by a woman's voice, cursing a streak that would have made the most hardened sailor blush.

"Is that...Lady Rutledge?" he asked, meeting the boy's eyes.

He shifted. "Yes, sir. It is, sir."

Cav let his eyes come shut a moment and shook his head. "I told her the troubles she would find with birds. Where is she then? Behind the stables?"

"Yes, sir. In the horse paddock," the young man said.

Cav was already heading out the door and waved his thanks as he did so. He didn't really need the direction. As he stepped out, Emily's shouts grew louder, and then she cried out, "Ouch!"

He ran then, racing around the stable, but when he reached the paddock, he came to a halt. Emily was standing in the middle of the training field, blonde hair tangled around her face, dress dirty, up to her ankles in mud as she swooped her hands at a half a dozen geese.

"Six geese a-laying," he muttered to himself with a half-smile. "Oh, Em."

"No wonder you are eaten!" she shouted at the birds. "You are the worst things with feathers God ever put on this earth. Go this way!"

She waved her hands again, and Cav chuckled as he vaulted over the paddock fence and into the field to join her. "Do you need help?"

He expected her to laugh as she realized he had joined her, to respond to this moment with her usual good-natured aplomb. But instead she pivoted, and he saw that her face was red, tears brightening her eyes, and she scowled at him.

"Go away, Cav," she grunted. "I've already made a mess of myself— I won't see anyone else do the same for my foolishness."

He took a step toward her despite her admonishment, and caught a glimpse of three footmen standing outside the fence, watching the entire exchange with worried expressions.

"You there, why are you not helping your lady?" Cav barked.

Emily staggered in the mud toward him and the cadre of geese hissed in unison. "Because I told them not to once I fell the third time. My boots may be filled with mud, but theirs ought not to be. Now *go away*."

He shook his head. "I am not going away, not when you are obviously upset. Not to mention surrounded by angry geese."

She waved her hands at the birds, and one of them struck his head toward her with a hiss. "They were supposed to be manageable! I wanted to put these little vests across their backs with egg decorations for the a-laying part." She held up a muddy piece of cloth with a beautifully embroidered egg on it. She balled it into her hand and shoved it at her side. "I worked on them for weeks after I got the idea for this party. But nothing is working and everything is terrible."

She huffed out a breath and turned her face, but not before he saw a tear slide down her cheek. And that was enough. He strode forward, waving his hands to scatter the angry geese, and caught her hand. "Come on, we'll escape."

"Escape?" she repeated, bright blue gaze finding his. "What do you mean?"

"I mean we'll have your horse saddled and stop the stable hand before he finishes with mine and we ride off for a little while. *Escape.*"

Her shoulders rolled forward. "But this is my party and everyone will be expecting a goose-related entertainment when they rise in a little while and—"

"Emily," he said, squeezing her hand and cutting her off from her rambling. She flushed and for a moment her fingers flexed against his. Seeking the comfort he offered.

"Very well," she whispered.

He drew her to the gate where the footmen were waiting and they were let out of the paddock. "Have her ladyship's horse readied and tell your man to keep mine saddled after all. Oh, and let the geese calm themselves down in the paddock. When we return, we'll decide if Lady Rutledge's plans are manageable." He glanced down at her. "And *you* come with me."

She acquiesced, following him into the warm stable. He led her to the back where a bench rested against one of the stalls and pointed to it. "Sit."

She did so, but glared up at him. "What are you doing?"

"You said your boots were full of mud," he said as he dropped to his knees before her, rather like he'd done when she was splayed out naked on the settee.

Clearly, she remembered the same thing, because she blushed and turned her face. Good. So she thought of yesterday too. That was something. "Y-you needn't trouble yourself," she said.

He arched a brow at her as he unfastened her bootstrap and gently tugged it free. "After all these years, you know that isn't true."

"I suppose not," she said, and she was watching him as he set her boot aside and wiped away the mud stuck to her stockinged foot. He pressed his thumb against the arch, massaging gently as he did so, and she gripped the edge of the bench with a quiet inhalation.

"You shouldn't do that here," she hissed.

"This?" he pressed, massaging a little harder. "I'm just warming up your cold feet, my lady."

"You aren't and you know it," she argued, but she didn't pull her foot away. She flexed against him, silently asking for more.

He chuckled and set her foot down, then dumped the remaining mud from her boot before he repeated the action on her opposite foot. As he did so, he said, "I'm impressed by your ability to swear, Emily. I don't think I've heard such creative pairings before, and I belong to several boxing clubs."

"Of course you do," she muttered beneath her breath. Then she shrugged. "I learned from the best. You and Andrew were quite loud when you peppered conversations over whisky with swearing."

"Hmmm, so it is our fault," he said. He held open her boot and she slid her foot in. He buckled it, choosing not to look at her as he said, "But what about the cause?"

She hesitated a moment. "Geese are frustrating."

He arched a brow at her. "That is an undeniable fact, but your ire seemed to stem from so much more."

She huffed out a breath. "You feel a need to dissect me then, Mr. Cavendish?"

He lifted up on his knees, wiping his hands clean on his trousers before he slid a finger beneath her chin and forced her to look at him. "Only to offer my support and friendship, Em. You know that."

Her lips parted slightly, and for a moment the air between them was thick with a tension that had never existed before. His desire had always been unrequited, unrecognized by her even as he struggled with it constantly. Now it was something different. Seeing it reflected in her eyes was overwhelming.

She swallowed hard, and then she nodded. "I know. I'm sorry. I'm out of sorts, but you don't deserve my wrath."

He shrugged as he put his attention on fastening her other boot.

Then he let her muddy skirts swish down around them and stood, holding out a hand to her.

"Tell me about it," he suggested. "Perhaps I can help."

They walked to the front of the stable together, and she smiled at her stablehand as he helped her up on a pretty sorrel mare named Jasmine she had favored for many years. She patted her flank and her tension seemed to bleed away. Cav remounted Hank, and they trotted off together at a gentle speed that didn't allow the brisk morning breeze to chill them too much.

"Is it really the geese, Emily?" he asked. "Are you going to try to tell me that it's only a flock of rude waterfowl that put you on the edge of tears?"

She worried her lip and glanced at him. "I would tell anyone else that but you. You have the annoying skill of knowing when I'm lying. But I feel foolish saying the truth."

"And what is that?" he pressed gently.

She was silent for a moment, and then she scrunched her face. "I'm going to sound foolish no matter how I say it, so here it is. I feel like a...failure."

He stared at her too long and nearly unseated himself. He managed to control Hank and keep his wits about him as he said, "How are you a failure?"

"My life is...out of control," she said. "It has been for a very long time. After all, I had plans, I had dreams and they were all stolen when Andrew died." She had that hint of sadness to her tone when she said his name, but it was softer now. Not so sharp or broken. "In the last few years, I've been in a kind of limbo. No longer in official mourning, but not ready to move on."

"You were pressured to do so, I know. I always respected your ability to hold true to your own heart," he said.

She gave him half a smile. "At least Andrew's family has been exceedingly kind about it. They've allowed me to continue on in our old home in London rather than moving to my new one. They've allowed me to treat Crossfox as a primary residence, as well, and have my parties here and sleep in the chamber that belongs to the viscountess."

"They adore you," he said softly, for he knew it was true.

"And I them. They will always mean a great deal to me. But I told you before that Andrew's brother is marrying."

"Yes," Cav said. "Gossip was already circulating before I arrived. Charles is marrying Phillipa Questington, isn't he?"

She nodded. "She's very sweet and has been nothing but lovely to me. They told me on Christmas Day that they will begin reading the bannes just after Epiphany, and I *am* happy for them. But..."

"But?"

Her sigh came shuddering out, and the sound was so painful that it nearly broke his heart. "This life I planned will become...theirs. This home and the one in London will be hers. I will be moving to my new residence when I return to the city. I'll come here, I'm sure—they are not a family of ogres and have made it clear I'll always have a place with them. But I'll only ever be their *guest*."

He gripped his reins tighter. Somehow he hadn't thought about the changes she was facing. The world had become hung up, stopped turning when Andrew died, at least for the two of them. The past five years had almost seemed out of time. But the bubble of that would burst, of course it would.

"How is that a failure, though, Emily?" he asked gently. "None of it is because of something you've done or not done."

"No, but I have struggled with losing these last vestiges of what I once believed would be my life." She shook her head. "Perhaps more than I let anyone, even you, know. And this party...it was supposed to help."

"Help?" he repeated. "How would it help?"

"I saw it as a way to say goodbye to this place, for one," she said, glancing over her shoulder toward the house that was now hidden in the distance. "But also I hoped...oh, it sounds so foolish now, I can't say it."

He pulled Hank up, stopping him on the trail, and she did the same with Jasmine. He turned the animal so he would face her. "Say it. It's me. You can say it."

Her gaze flitted over him, and how he wished he could read her mind, because her expression was clouded with so much emotion that he couldn't parse out what it all was and name it so he could react properly. She was a flood of everything and he could only watch.

"I hoped that by matching my guests, my *victims* as you keep putting it, that I would let loose some of the love I've had bottled up in me. That I'd see something I nurtured grow into that beautiful thing I lost. And somehow it would give me peace."

"Emily," he said softly.

"Don't," she whispered, and slung herself off the horse. She walked off into the glade just off the path where they had stopped, her boots crunching on the frozen, dead grass. "Don't play or tease right now."

He slowly dismounted, careful as he approached her. He let his hand close around her forearm, and then he rested his chin on the crown of her head. After a moment's hesitation, she relaxed back against him, soft against him as she allowed hm to hold her.

"I would never tease you about something so important," he said. "I didn't know how much this matchmaking meant to you. I'm sorry if you felt I was too playful."

"I lo—" She cut herself off and went stiff against his chest. "I like that you're playful. Sometimes it was the only thing that saved me all these years. You must admit that I'm making a muck of everything, though."

"The matches," he said carefully.

She nodded, and he loved the slide of the crown of her head against his chin just before she glided from his arms and turned to face him. Like the intimacy of him holding her had become too much in that moment. "No one is connecting, no matter how I slide them around toward each other. The Mulberry twins hide out in their chamber half the time, Lady Abigail stands to the side, just watching everyone. Lady Thea despises Lord Allington so much that it seems to dominate any room they are in together. I cannot…fix it. Hence, I feel like a failure."

He shook his head. "You have all the best intentions, and who could not adore you for them? But love isn't a project that can be fixed. Trust me."

Her brow wrinkled at that statement and he hurried to continue so she wouldn't question him further on the topic. "You have set a handful of people into a room together and given them a reason to decide if they like each other. If they don't, it's because they don't spark that feeling. It isn't because you could have done something different."

"I suppose that's true," she said with a sigh. "Leave it to you to give me good advice. I despise you for it."

He couldn't help but grin at that. When she said it, it lifted some of the tension between them and he felt like their friendship was back to normal.

"I will try to retreat as swiftly as possible back to being yet another mess you manage, my lady," he said with a little bow. "I would not wish to shock you by becoming wise."

Her smile faltered. "You've always been wise, Cav. And I've never seen you as a mess I managed." She shifted. "But I suppose now is as good a time as any to address the final matter that is troubling me."

His stomach sank at the way she worried her hands before her. "You and me?" he said, wanting to be the one who said it first.

She nodded slowly. "What happened between us yesterday."

"Regrets?"

"No," she said, so swiftly and firmly that it caught him off guard. Pleased him, but caught him off guard.

"Good," he said softly. He moved toward her a long step and saw her tremble in response. Her gaze flitted over him in one long sweep, and she blushed. "Then what do you want to talk to me about?"

"Cav, I don't think it's wise if we repeat it, as wonderful as it was."

The words were like arrows and they pierced his heart. But he had to pretend they meant nothing. After all, he had expected them. He had been aware of his love and desire for years. But if she felt any of it, if there was any chance for them, this was all new to her. She would fight it. Fear it. Analyze it.

"Why is that?" he asked. "I ask because I have a vested interest in repeating it."

Her eyes went wide. "You—you want to take me to bed again?"

He shrugged one shoulder, making his reaction nonchalant when it most definitely wasn't. "I very much enjoyed it, Emily. I have thought of very little else since. If we both received pleasure, then how is it any different than when we play a hand of whist together or laugh over some joke or take a ride around your estate?"

She folded her arms. "It is very different and you of all people should know it."

"Me of all people," he asked, and now he didn't have to fake confusion.

"You have had so many lovers," she huffed.

He stared at her for a moment and had to fight the urge to laugh in her face. There was certainly no way to explain to her that his mad game of taking women to his bed had always been a way to forget the one woman he couldn't have. Or to explain that it had been years...*years*...since he played that game. Since Andrew died and his main concern had become Emily. Always Emily. Forever Emily. Whatever front he put on to the world, to his friends, never extended beyond bluster anymore.

"I thought you said rakes had advantages," he said. "Isn't that why you invited so many of us to your matchmaking party?"

She sighed but didn't rise to his bait. Instead, she moved forward and surprised him by taking his gloved hands in her own. She stared up into his face and he felt like she could see down to the very soul of him.

"You are my best friend," she whispered. "I may have other friends or Andrew's family, but when it comes to what is really important, you are all I have. So no matter how much I enjoyed what we did, I fear that if it ruins things between us, it will have too high a price for pleasure."

He set his jaw. How much he wanted to confess his love to her right here and now in the freezing cold when she was still muddy and flustered and perfect in every way he could imagine. Only her resistance wouldn't allow it. He knew what would happen then. She would panic, not ready for what he wanted, what he offered.

But if he eased her into it…if he took the passion she seemed ready to accept if only she could give herself permission…well, that was one way to get closer to her heart. A way to make her think about a future that could mean everything.

He lifted his hand away from hers and traced the fullness of her bottom lip with his thumb. She shivered at the action.

"Don't you know you're all I have, too?" he asked. "That I would never risk our friendship just for pleasure? I think we can have both."

"Said just like a man," she said, and she smiled up at him.

He returned the expression. "When I touch you, I see you react, Emily. I'm not a fool. Do you deny it?"

She shook her head after a long hesitation.

"Then why reject it?" he asked. "Why keep yourself from pleasure if we can promise not to let it spoil what we already have?"

She worried her lip gently and how he longed to lean down and nip it. He somehow maintained control and waited for her response.

"Are you talking about an affair?" she asked slowly. "Something limited?"

He frowned. Even if this was the door into her heart, the way he might find what he truly desired, her resistance still stung. Understanding it and reveling in it were two distinct things.

"If you'd like," he croaked. "We could say it only lasts during the party. And then see if we wanted it to be longer when we return to London."

Having that boundary seemed to bleed the tension away from her entire being. "I suppose that is an intelligent way to do things, if we were to consider it," she said slowly. "But I'd want a few…rules."

"Rules," he repeated, and had to laugh. "Of course you do. What are they, then?"

"My private parlor is a fine place for us to meet, but *not* in the master bedroom," she said.

"I would not wish to bed you there, either. I would point out though, that the chamber you have provided for me has a very nice bed, versus wedging ourselves onto your settee, if you would prefer."

"Oh, yes," she said with a blush. "That does make sense. Your chamber then."

"What else?"

"You cannot…distract me…when we're not in the chamber. We're only friends when we're in my public halls, around other people. There are enough rumors about us circulating, I would not want to create more with some unintended touch or look."

He nodded, but it was difficult. After all, he had built the last five years on stolen glances and grazing touch. She just hadn't noticed it.

"I will agree to that." He took her hand. "And I have a rule of my own."

She looked down at their interlacing fingers and then back up to his face with a swallow. "What is that?"

"No guilt," he said softly. "If you don't want me to do something, you'll tell me and I'll stop. But what we do together, in the privacy of my chamber or any other, cannot make you toss and turn at night and tell yourself you've done something wrong."

A flutter of a smile tilted her lips. "You do know me so well."

"I can use that to your benefit," he promised.

She let out another of those telling shivers, even as pink suffused her cheeks. She drew a few long breaths before she said, "Then…*yes.*"

"Yes?" he repeated, almost unsure he'd truly heard that. Could this be yet another dream?

"If we can agree that we don't lose our friendship, that we limit this to our time here and the other rules we've laid out, I think we could still…connect as we did."

"A bargain like this must be sealed with a kiss," he said, and tugged her a little closer.

Her breath came out in a tiny cloud of heat against the cold, but she didn't pull away. Instead she lifted her lips toward his and gave a muffled sigh when he took them.

His arms came around her, he memorized the feel of her there, soft and warm and his, at least for a little while. Hopefully long enough to show her that a future was possible. And he let her go before she pushed back.

"I would do more of that," he explained, "But I believe that breaks your 'not outside my chamber' rule."

Her eyes were wide and glazed. "I suppose it does."

"Shall we ride back?" he asked, motioning to their mounts. "And see how the geese have recovered?"

She blinked. "Blimey, I forgot all about the geese."

He laughed as he took her back to the animals and helped her seat herself. As he swung up on Hank, he said, "Then I've done my job."

"You always do," she said as they turned back toward the house and trotted on. "Thank you. Thank you for always being...you."

He smiled, and the rest of the ride he forced himself to talk to her about topics with less emotional charge. He had won a battle today, though certainly not the war. But he'd seen a path to the conclusion he wished for.

And taking the route through passion certainly wasn't the worst way to convince a lady to fall in love.

CHAPTER 9

The final hours of the year were held in traditional fashion, gathered in Emily's parlor, the guests telling stories of the months past, making shadow puppets on the wall and doing shadow portraits of each other. And in any normal circumstances, she would have considered it a success after the morning's terrible start. No one had even mentioned the lack of geese a-laying and had only cooed and complimented her on her goose egg embroidery that now decorated the room.

Cav's idea, of course. And he'd been the first to point out the pieces and make a great fanfare about how they were the perfect celebration for the geese a-laying. He always knew how to come to her rescue, though. He had been doing it for a very long time. Even before Andrew's death, Cav had been her friend and her protector.

And now he wanted to be…more. Or at least, something different. Her lover, if only temporarily. She shivered at the thought and tracked him as he crossed the room to refill his glass with his favorite red wine. She always made sure she had bottles upon bottles of it on hand for his visits.

He glanced at her, and when he found her staring, he gave her a little look. A rather heavy glance that spoke volumes without him having to say a word.

You're breaking your own rules, Emily. She could practically hear him saying that right against her ear as his big hands slid along her arms. That phantom voice wasn't wrong, either. She had been the one to declare they ought not moon over each other in public, and yet she couldn't take her eyes off him.

He, on the other hand, seemed to have no trouble sticking to the boundaries she had staked out for herself. Aside from his pointed glance in her direction, he had hardly acknowledged her beyond what was needed for polite discourse since their return from their ride.

Why that annoyed her when it was exactly what she wanted—no, *needed*—was a question, indeed.

"That gown is stunning, Lady Rutledge."

Emily jolted, for she'd been so wrapped up in her musings over Cav she hadn't even noticed that Prudence Mulberry had slipped up beside her.

"Thank you." She glanced down at the dress. It was a dark pink silk with a lace overlay and beaded sleeves and a beaded floral pattern along the hem. "It is one of my favorites."

She wrinkled her brow as she said it, because she realized Cav had said that exact thing, that the dress was his favorite, the last time she wore it. That had been a month ago in London when she had come to have supper with him and a few other friends.

She cleared her throat. "Are you enjoying the party, Lady Prudence?"

Prudence tilted her head. "How did you know it was me and not my sister?"

Emily smiled. "I made note of the rings you and Lady Honoria wear. You wear yours on your right hand, she on her left."

Prudence blinked. "There are few who make such an effort to determine our identity. It is much appreciated."

Emily patted her hand. The twins had been removing themselves from so many activities, it was nice to connect to at least one of them.

"To answer your question," Prudence continued, this time with a little more friendliness to her tone. "I *am* enjoying the party. My sister and I are a quiet sort, I know. I would much rather be reading or sewing than doing such lively activities. But I suppose one must get used to such things. Our mother would very much like to see us wed, I think."

They both glanced across the room to where Lady Mulberry was standing with Cav and a few of the other gentlemen. There was no denying the look of the hunt in her sharp eyes. Prudence flinched.

"Well, perhaps you're on your way with this gathering," Emily said gently. "There are a few days left still. Is there no gentleman who has caught your eye?"

Prudence glanced again at where her mother stood. Lord Weatherall and Adrian Powell were the other men standing alongside Cav. Emily twisted her mouth. She'd seated Prudence next to Mr. Powell at a luncheon earlier in the week and she hadn't seemed particularly interested. But Allington was a possibility. She'd matched him with Honoria, not Prudence, with no success.

"Mr. Cavendish is a very handsome sort," Prudence said.

Emily blinked a few times. What an odd sensation rushed through her with those benign words. Like Prudence had shoved her under water and now everything sounded far away and tinny.

"Mr. Cavendish," she repeated. "Yes, he certainly is that."

She was struggling for something else to say, for some way to control the unexpected negative emotions that bubbled up in her at the idea that Prudence Mulberry would look at Cav and see a future. Jealousy. That's what it felt like even though that couldn't be right. She and Cav were friends, she wanted him to be happy. The fact that they'd become lovers couldn't have possibly changed that.

She was lucky that before she had to find the answers, Cringle appeared in the parlor door and rang a small bell. She nodded at him.

"It seems it is almost time to welcome the new year!" she proclaimed with an apologetic smile for Prudence as she stepped away. "Let us make a circle and I will prepare to open the window to let the old out and the new in!"

The crowd was playful, laughing as they joined hands in a circle in the middle of the large room. They watched the clock on the mantel together as the seconds ticked down. When only ten remained, they began the countdown.

"Ten, nine, eight, seven, six..." She counted along with the group and found Cav in the crowd. He might have now been holding hands with Prudence Mulberry and her mother, but he was watching Emily. She flushed as she put her hand on the sash to open the window. "...three, two, one!"

She threw open the window, and a blast of cold spun into the room as the group began to sing "Auld Lang Syne" together. She sang along, feeling every word about this song about the importance of friendship. But when Cav smiled at her, it wasn't friendship she felt curling her toes in her slippers. It was desire.

She pushed it away and finished the song, then swiftly shut the window and hustled to the fire to warm her hands there as the party toasted and went back to their games and drinks and conversations.

She sighed as she watched the flames and tried to ignore Cav's presence at her back. At last 1813 had come to an end. And 1814 had begun. A new year with new possibilities. And for the first time since Andrew's death she found herself excited to see what a new year would hold for her.

~

C av walked through the darkened halls toward his bedchamber. The party had broken up late, after three, and the rest had gone to their beds. He had stayed up a few moments longer, finishing his whisky and staring out at the clear, cold, starry sky.

A new year was always an exciting time. But this one thrilled and terrified him more than most. After all, he'd begun something new with Emily. He knew, just as she feared, that it would change everything between them. Watching her tonight in that gorgeous dark pink gown, smiling and laughing with her guests, bright and alive and beautiful...all the love had swelled in him, a prison and a gateway all at once.

If only it were returned.

He sighed as he reached his room and pushed open the door. It was so late, he hated to wake his valet, so he walked to the fire and tossed a log onto the flames to lift the light so he could undress. As he did so, he heard the sound of a throat being cleared from the direction of his bed.

He turned slowly and found Emily sitting on the bench at the foot of the bed. She was watching him and as he moved toward her, she staggered to her feet.

"Cav—" she began. She cut herself off and dug into her pocket. What she retrieved was a sprig of mistletoe. With a nervous smile, she lifted it over her head. "I thought we might—"

He caught her words with his lips.

As the mistletoe fluttered to the floor behind him, she wrapped her arms around his neck, lifting into his chest with a muffled moan that seemed to wend into his bloodstream and go straight into his cock.

She pulled her mouth from his just a fraction, just a breath and whispered, "Happy New Year."

He smiled, drinking in the sight of her in the firelight. "Happy New Year."

Then he dipped his mouth and kissed her again as his fingers found the back of her gown. They were quiet except for the sounds of their mouths meeting as he unfastened her, careful with the pretty dress as he lowered it down her arms, her hips. He gathered it up as it pooled around her feet and stepped away just long enough to drape it over the back of a chair.

She laughed as he returned to her, but the laughter faded as he let his gaze slide over her. Her underthings were pink like the dress. The fabric was so delicate it was almost sheer, and he saw the shadow of her hard nipples, the triangle of her pubic hair beneath the satin. He reached for her, cupping her hips, letting his fingers slide with just the thin layer between them as she reached back to grip the edge of his bed for purchase.

"Cav," she whispered. It was a plea. It was a demand.

He tugged her flush against him and lifted her up on the high bed, stepping between her legs. She was no longer shorter than he was now that she sat up on the edge. Their mouths were even and he took advantage, kissing her as he pulled the strap of her chemise down to her elbow. The fabric dropped forward and he groaned his approval as he looked down at the beautiful breast he had just revealed.

He bent his head, swirling his tongue around impossibly soft flesh, tugging her hard nipple between his teeth as she threw her head back with a cry.

He sucked harder, harder, loving how her hips lifted against his, grinding to find the release he would give. The fact that she was eager as he was made his heart sing and his body throb.

He pulled the other strap down and dragged his mouth across her chest. She dug her fingers into his hair, demanding pleasure as her nails raked his scalp. He acquiesced, laving her opposite nipple with as much focus as he had the first.

Her chemise drooped around her waist, and she lifted her backside so he could pull it free. He tossed it over his shoulder and stepped back. Great God, but this woman. She was so intensely beautiful with her full curves and blonde hair half fallen from the pretty style she'd worn earlier in the evening. Her lips were pink from kissing. He wanted to make her entire body that same color from his tongue and stubble and hands. He wanted to taste every inch of her.

She pushed herself back on the bed and lounged on his pillows as she watched him through a hooded gaze. "Undress, Cavendish. I want to see you."

Cav had read the term *knees went weak* in many a book he'd shared with Emily over the years. She loved a romantic tale, after all, and he indulged her and enjoyed those stories as much as she did. But he'd never experienced the sensation until this very moment. She gave that calm, almost casual order, and his knees trembled.

"Yes, my lady. At your service," he said with a small salute before he shrugged out of his jacket and then unwound his cravat slowly.

When he tugged his shirt over his head, all her pretense of being bored and unaffected went away. She sat up on her elbows and reached for him. He moved closer and hissed out a breath as her fingers dragged down his chest.

She lifted her gaze to him. "You like when I touch you."

"Very much," he agreed.

She leaned closer, pushing up on her knees and pressed her lips to the wings of his collarbone. Her tongue traced there, then she dragged lower, over his pectoral, across to the other, teasing him like he had teased her. The reaction was the same. He grunted her name, trying to remember anything else in the world beyond the pleasure of her touch. If he only focused on that, he might spend before he buried himself in her, and that wasn't the way to start a new year.

He unfastened his fall front as she licked his chest, dragged her mouth down his abdomen. Her eyes widened as he freed his cock and pushed his trousers away. She caught his length and stroked him, her face tantalizingly close. Then she looked up at him with a wickedness he'd never seen in her before.

"Could I make you lose control, Cav?" she whispered. "Do I have that power?"

He nodded slowly, for there was no denying the truth. "You do."

She bent her head and nuzzled his cock with her cheek. He jolted at the spike of pleasure that drove upward into his balls, edging to the point of pain, to the place where his vision blurred. He fought for purchase, tried to remember how to speak so he could say her name, but before he could, she darted out her tongue and traced the head of him.

"Fuck," he grunted, hating himself for exposing her to such bawdy language but unable to keep the curse from escaping his lips.

She chuckled as she sucked him between her lips, and the vibration made him push even farther into the wet, hot cavern of her mouth. She took him without resistance, without hesitation, swirling her tongue around him once, twice. She stroked him, taking him deeper with every thrust.

Some ladies didn't like this act. But she seemed to revel in it. She glanced up at him as she pleasured him, watching his face, her blue eyes glittering in the firelight as she drove him toward the edge of reason.

He didn't want to fall over that edge before he dragged her with him. And it was only because of that thought that he managed to pull from her lips. He tumbled her backward across the bed. He caught her calves, dragging her to the edge of the mattress, and then he dropped his mouth to her sex, tormenting her as she had tormented him.

She tasted so sweet. So perfect. He never wanted any flavor but hers on his lips until the day he drew his last breath. He licked and sucked and felt her quicken beneath him as she moaned and whispered his name and ground up against him in a torrent of unleashed desire that overwhelmed him and made him hope.

He ignored the hope. It was too dangerous now. He dove into the desire instead. The pleasure of feeling the waves of her release begin against his tongue. She lifted into him with a cry and he drew her through it, feeling the ripples against his tongue as she thrashed. And just as the waves subsided, he pushed her legs wider, stood to his full height and slid his cock into her to the hilt.

She gasped and the ripples of her release increased. She milked him as he thrust, devouring her mouth as he had devoured her sex. All the mattered in that moment was the joining of their bodies, the mingling of their sweat, the way she dug her nails into his shoulders as she came in a gasping, gripping crescendo.

It was too much for him. It was everything. He shut his eyes, focusing only on the feel of her around him, the tightening of his balls as he neared release.

When it overtook him, he withdrew from her, sucking her tongue so he wouldn't declare his love for her as he came between them and then collapsed over her.

He waited for her to speak. Emily always had something to say. But she didn't. She just curled herself into him, letting him wrap his arms around her as she settled her head into his shoulder.

"Don't let me stay too long," she whispered into his neck.

He nodded. "I'll stay awake," he promised.

And he meant it. There would be no way he'd sleep now as he held her, a fantasy come true. He didn't want to sleep. This was the dream and he was living it. He would take it as long as he could.

So as she drifted off to sleep, her hand fisted against his heart, he pressed a kiss to her temple and reveled in this moment. He could only hope there would be more of them. And that this new year would mean a new beginning for them together.

CHAPTER 10

SEVEN SWANS A-SWIMMING

E mily stood on the bridge overlooking the lake and smiled at her party in the distance. They were ice skating today, gliding over the frozen waters and occasionally startling the swans that represented their seventh day of Christmas.

It was the perfect moment, something out of a painting. And yet she did not feel at ease. Cav had woken her just before dawn from a sleep better than any she'd had since Andrew's death. He'd made love to her slowly and gently and then sent her on her way. She'd paced her room the rest of the morning, reliving every touch, every moment they'd shared.

And hating herself for wanting more and more and more of those moments. She glanced down. Her gloves were so fitted, she could see the circle of her ring beneath the leather.

She flinched and brushed the raised ridge with her thumb as she found Cav in the crowd. His greatcoat flapped around his toned calves as he managed an awkward spin that made the rest of the group clap and whoop with support. He was smiling, and she found herself doing the same.

"Might I join you, Lady Rutledge?"

Emily started. Over and over again she lost herself staring at a man she'd considered a friend and declared a temporary lover. It was unseemly and she had to force a smile for Lady Hickson as she glided off the ice and awkwardly walked on her skates to stand on the bridge beside Emily.

"You are quite good, Virginia," Emily said. "I saw you doing pirouettes that would have put anyone to shame."

"I've always enjoyed skating," Virginia said. "My father has a lake on his country estate and he would drag me out there all winter long every year while he...well, he had things to entertain him there. And I would skate and skate and skate forever."

There was something troubled in Virginia's tone, and while Emily considered them friendly acquaintances, she didn't know the woman well enough to pry. Nor did Virginia seem open to sharing more.

They both turned their attention to the ice again, and Emily smiled as Cav glided around. Her smile fell when Lady Abigail approached him. She, unlike Virginia, was not an expert on skates, and Cav caught her as she slid and slipped. They were both laughing. A twinge of jealousy she ought not feel made Emily grip the wooden edge of the bridge harder.

"You and Cavendish seem close as ever," Virginia said softly.

Emily jerked her face toward her and saw Virginia was watching her watch Cav. She blushed and wished she hadn't. "He's an old friend," she said.

Virginia nodded slowly. "That is always the best match, it seems."

Emily winced. Here she had been operating under the assumption it was rakes and wallflowers that were the best match. Now she wasn't certain she understood anything when it came to attraction or desire or love. Her entire world had been turned on its head, after all.

She let out a long breath. Behind the crowd, two of the swans had moved to the shore. They were wandering together, close to each other's sides. From the angle she and Virginia were standing, they almost looked like their wings were clasped, even though that wasn't possible.

"Swans mate for life, you know," she mused softly.

For a long beat, Virginia didn't answer. But finally she said, "Sometimes."

Emily wrinkled her brow. "What do you mean?"

"My father was obsessed with ornithology, along with a great many other things. And apparently there are cases of swan separation. Even divorce."

Emily couldn't help but laugh at the idea of a bird divorce. "Scandalous!"

Virginia giggled along with her. "And there's also—"

She cut herself off with a blush and her expression made Emily's stomach sink. "Also what?" she pressed.

Virginia shook her head. "You've been a kind hostess and I would not wish to offend you."

"How would the topic of swan husbandry offend me?" Emily asked.

"Because you and I had very different circumstances in our marriage," Virginia said. "It is well known you and Rutledge were a love match. So certain topics may be more painful for you."

Emily shifted slightly. "What is the other reason you have for swans not mating for life?"

Virginia faced her straight on. "Widowed swans often go on to make new matches."

Emily found herself glancing out at Cav again. He was still with Lady Abigail and they were talking away from the rest of the group. She was very pretty. Emily didn't want to care about that. She didn't want to care at all.

"I hope that will be true for you," she forced herself to say.

Virginia watched her closely for a moment and then nodded. "Perhaps." She turned aside and watched the crowd again. "Either way, I suppose Cavendish will certainly marry soon."

Emily swallowed hard. "You—you are the second person to make that statement to me during this party. I wonder where the rumors are originating from."

"Everywhere," Virginia said gently. "It is on the lips of nearly every mama or chaperone preparing their soon-to-be-minted Diamonds of the First Water. He is of an age, is he not? And certainly it is expected of him to wed, he has his fortune to protect and his family line."

All those things were very true. Emily could find no way to deny them, not that she should. She'd always known Cav would wed, hadn't she? Even in these last few years when she'd depended so heavily on him, she had thought about who might make him a good bride...hadn't she?

She must have. A good friend would do so. She was his good friend. That they'd started an affair had nothing to do with anything.

"I suppose he's always enjoyed his bachelorhood so much, it's hard to picture him settled," Emily said. Lied. She could very easily picture him reading out a book with someone he loved. Or strolling through a garden patiently scribbling down every note about every flower. Or any of the other dozens of things he'd done with her.

"You mean his reputation as a rake?" Virginia asked. She glanced off toward Cav and shook her head. "I don't know. I mean, we've all heard the stories. He's boisterous and playful and sometimes a tiny bit inappropriate. And he'd had his share of widows and actresses, I suppose. But never a mistress. The tales of his conquests have... quieted in the last few years especially."

Emily bent her head and stared at her hands, clenched along the bridge top. "He's been busy, I suppose."

"Do you think it's that or—"

Emily jolted, for she was certain Virginia was about to point out the connection Emily couldn't bear to consider at present. To keep that from happening, she straightened up. "It looks as though the others are motioning to us to join them. I need to put on my skates, but you shouldn't wait for me."

Virginia looked at her, and Emily thought there was a modicum of pity in her eyes as she did so. Then she squeezed Emily's hand gently. "Of course."

Emily could say nothing else as Virginia eased her way back on the ice. She forced herself to put her back to the others as she put on her own skates. This was exactly what she'd feared when she agreed to Cav's suggestion that they could share pleasure but not endanger their friendship. A reasonable, rational woman would walk away. Would allow him the future he deserved.

Only she didn't feel particularly rational or reasonable as she glided onto the ice toward the others. Toward Cav and Abigail, who still had their heads together as they skated. What she was going to do, she had no idea. But certainly, it would be a rational, reasonable response. She could not lose her head. She would not.

~

Cav wasn't the best of ice skaters, but he did enjoy it. And compared to some of Emily's other guests, he was proficient. Even now Lady Abigail, who had staggered into him as she attempted even the simplest movement across the frozen water, clung to his arm, laughing.

Abigail was a lovely woman, with dark hair and brown eyes. She had a nice smile. In other circumstances, he might have been enchanted by the press of her hand on the crook of his elbow. The sound of her laughter echoing in the winter air.

Instead, he found himself watching Emily as she stood on the bridge where the stream fed into the lake. She was standing with Lady Hickson and looked very serious as they chatted. He could tell by the way her fingers flexed open and shut on the railing. Always a tell that she was troubled. Because of him? Because of something else?

"You know, Mr. Cavendish, any other lady might be offended not to have a gentleman's full attention in a moment like this."

He jolted at Lady Abigail's voice and glanced down to find her watching him with a knowing gaze. "I apologize, my lady," he said. "I was woolgathering. A foolish endeavor when one is balanced on a sliver of metal. And when in such good company."

She smiled. "You needn't apologize. It is evident you are distracted by Lady Rutledge. As you often are, I have observed."

He felt his nostrils flare a fraction and tried to otherwise keep his reaction from his face. "Lady Rutledge and I are friends. I suppose I am sometimes concerned about her well-being."

"Certainly," Lady Abigail said. "As any good friend would be. There is also the fact you are in love with her."

Cav nearly deposited himself on his arse on the ice, he was so taken aback by that statement. Many danced around this subject, trying to pry into something they didn't understand or couldn't fathom. But Lady Abigail said those words as if they were nothing, rather than swords to Cav's heart.

He cleared his throat. "I—"

She shrugged. "No need to come up with some retort. I am very well versed in longing, sir. I recognize it when I see it."

He shifted his attention back to her. Though she was smiling, he saw the flicker of pain in Lady Abigail's expression. And like her, he recognized a kindred spirit in heartbreak.

"I see," he said.

"And you needn't worry. I would not speak of it to anyone else," she continued.

He swallowed. There had never been anyone in his life to talk to about his feelings. Andrew had been his closest friend, and there was no way to broach the subject of Cav's unrequited love for Emily without destroying everything. His grandfather knew, but his grandfather was always about action, not reflection. Hence his statement a few weeks earlier that this might be Cav's last chance.

"I suppose," he said slowly, feeling out how the words fell from his lips. "That my feelings may be deeper."

"But she is resistant," Abigail said softly. "Because of her marriage to your late friend, I assume?"

He nodded. "Very much so."

She let out her breath in a long sigh. "I am sorry, Cavendish."

"I appreciate it. Though I have put myself in this situation, haven't I? By continuing to keep her close. By hoping against hope that one day things may change."

"And will they?" Abigail pressed.

He worried his lip a moment. "I honestly don't know. I make progress sometimes." He thought of holding Emily in his arms all night. Of waking her with kisses. Of her smile before she left his bed. But now she wasn't even looking at him. She pulled so far back that he almost couldn't see her. "But then..."

"If you cannot win her, that would make things difficult for you. It would be unfair to your future bride."

He bent his head. "I have considered that. Even if I only entered into a marriage of convenience, I do not think any wife would like my friendship with the love of my life. It would hurt her. But the alternative is losing the friendship, which does mean the world to me."

Abigail turned toward him, and suddenly her dark eyes were lit up. "What if you picked someone who wouldn't care that you pined? Who also couldn't have what they wanted?" As the said the last, she glanced across the ice to where her lady's companion was standing with Adrian Powell. For a moment, he thought Abigail might like the industrialist, and he could see no reason why she would not be able to pursue her heart.

Then Powell stepped away, but Abigail's gaze remained firmly affixed on her companion.

Cav's eyes went wide as understanding dawned. "Ah. I see."

Abigail narrowed her gaze. "Would that anger you, that your wife was attracted in a different direction? Would you...punish her for her heart?"

"Never," he said, and touched her hand. "We cannot choose who we are. Who we love. I know that better than anyone. But are you truly suggesting we could make a marriage of convenience that would never be expected to change?"

"Yes. A business arrangement. I would even bear your children. We could find a way to make that work. And I would not care if you loved Lady Rutledge until the day you were cold in the grave. I would assume you would feel the same way about me."

Cav could scarcely believe this conversation. Abigail did not hesitate, it seemed. And her offer *could* actually work. He looked at her face again. She seemed very pained and pity flooded him, for he knew that heartbreak all too well.

"Does she know how you feel?" he asked gently.

She blinked. "No. She does not share my inclination, so why tell her?"

He nodded. "I'm sorry."

"Would you consider my suggestion? It could serve us both well." Abigail pressed.

"I might consider it," he said. "If I couldn't be happy with Emily in my future."

Relief flooded her features. "Good. Although I tend to think you might have a better chance than I."

"Why is that?" he asked, wrinkling his brow.

She jerked her head toward the area behind him. "Because she's coming over now—and she looks jealous."

He pivoted and watched as Emily jerked and slipped her way across the ice toward him. There was an expression of dark determination on her face as she went, a stormy sea of emotion that almost made him smile.

"Do you need assistance?" he called out.

"No, you are helping Lady Abigail," she answered, and he thought she put the slightest emphasis on her name as Emily's eyes narrowed. "I will manage. Though I think this is an excellent time to change pairings! Gentlemen, find a lady who you have not yet spent time with and let us all take a turn around the lake."

She jerked away. He supposed she was trying to look haughty or in control as she did it. Instead, she nearly flipped herself onto her backside and only barely kept on her feet.

Abigail laughed and gave him a wink as she skated past him to find a new partner. "Good luck, Mr. Cavendish."

"Wait! Lady Abigail?"

She stopped on unsteady feet and faced him. "Yes?"

"I am the worst one to give advice on this matter since I obviously have no sense of anything when it comes to the heart. But if your companion doesn't share your inclination, if you truly have no chance, I hope you won't give up on the notion entirely. And if we were to come to some arrangement..." He cleared his throat, for this was the most odd and awkward conversation ever to be held on ice or land. "I would hope you would seek out company elsewhere."

Her expression softened. "Well, that is a lovely sentiment, sir. I will think of it."

She skated off, and Cav pivoted. Emily had also found a partner, but it was one of the chaperones. They were supporting each other while she laughed. But he thought it was strained.

And the fact that she didn't like him connecting to another lady gave him more hope than he should dare have. Now to figure out what to do with that.

CHAPTER 11

Cav stepped into his chamber after luncheon had ended, intent
on catching up on some of the sleep he had lost the night
before as he reveled in holding Emily. But the moment he closed the
door, he could see that wasn't going to happen. Because she was
standing at his window and turned to face him as he entered.

She had changed after skating to another of his favorite frocks, a
dark blue silk that turned her eyes to sapphires. She stood with the
light framing her, looking like an angel sent to both soothe and
torment him.

She shifted and blushed as he reached back to lock the door
behind him and leaned against it. "I wasn't expecting you, my lady."

"Does it follow that I am unwelcome?" she asked, and he heard the
tremble in her voice.

"You are always welcome." He pushed off the door and came a step
closer. "Always."

She glanced down at her feet. "I had forgotten how good you were
on skates."

"You are too, once you got out on the ice," he said. "How long has it
been since we did this last?"

"Since before Andrew died. Christmas of...was it six years ago?"

He sucked in a breath as memories bombarded him. "Has it been so long? Was that the year he kept falling on his arse?"

"Yes." She giggled, and it lit her face as she finally met his eyes. "He was trying to act like it was on purpose, but we both knew he was just terrible at it." They were both quiet a moment, and then she cleared his throat. "You were very popular with the ladies today, though."

He arched a brow. Abigail had made the observation that Emily was jealous and though she kept her tone even, he saw the flicker of emotion in her eyes. The way her hands clenched at her sides even as she pretended to be making small talk.

"I suppose," he said with a shrug.

"Abigail took up your attention for a very long time," she continued. She'd begun to smooth the front of her gown, little fluttering movements.

"Oh yes," he said. "She's a lovely woman. I hadn't had the opportunity to spend much time with her over the years, but she is something." He felt cruel to stoke the fire of Emily's discomfort, but then again, it might be just what she needed to see the future he saw. To accept the life he wanted to offer to her on a silver platter.

"She is," she said. "She is. Looking for a marriage, I think."

He thought of Abigail's offer of a loveless union, of her despair when she looked at her companion. The sting of unrequited love would certainly cement their friendship if they did come to an arrangement.

"I suppose she is," he said carefully. "It's expected of her, I think."

"And of you," Emily said, and there was another tremor to her voice. "Apparently sooner rather than later. And why not? After all, you have a fine future and you'll certainly want to create a few heirs to carry it on and—"

He didn't let her finish. He couldn't listen to her prattle on about marrying someone else when she was standing there next to his bed, looking so beautiful that he almost had to turn away from her.

Instead he crossed the room in three long steps and caught her in his arms, dropping his mouth to hers. She opened immediately, wrapping her arms around his neck, clinging there with the same desperation he felt burning inside his chest. At least they shared that, even if she might deny him anything else.

He'd take this for now, feed from it. Cling to it until he was forced away. Pray it would be enough.

He shoved those thoughts away and began to unbutton her pretty dress. She hissed out a sound of pleasure against his lips as he slid his hands into the gap he created, beneath her chemise, against her bare skin. He raked his nails there gently, and she arched against him.

"Oh God," she murmured, turning her mouth into his throat, sucking at his skin until his vision blurred.

He tugged the dress and chemise down together, and then stepped back to look at her. The fabric drooped at her waist, revealing the gorgeous expanse of her skin, the swell of her breasts that he wanted to worship for the rest of his life.

He reached for her, dragging the back of his hand against her flesh. She caught his hand and turned it, forcing him to fully cup her. He smiled at her ardor, her silent demand. And he so wanted to fulfill it. Fulfill her without her having to expend any effort beyond accepting.

But they were running out of time now. Less than a week remained of her party, and back in London it would be too easy for her to convince herself that they needed to fall back into their old habits, their past relationship. He needed her to surrender, or at least start to surrender, to the idea of more.

Which meant he had to make her begin to admit it.

"Tell me what you want, Emily."

She blinked at him. "I think it's obvious, isn't it?"

He chuckled as she arched into him again and her nipple brushed his palm. "Tell me, not show me."

Her jaw set, and he realized she was gritting her teeth. He stood firm, waiting for her. Hoping she would give him just this inch, praying it would be the first of many that would bring them closer than friendship, closer than sex.

If only she would just say the words.

～

E mily couldn't breathe as she stood there, eyes screwed shut, feeling Cav waiting for her. Saying what she wanted felt so damned intimate. It felt so vulnerable. It felt...it felt like a point of no return.

Was she ready for no return?

"I want," she whispered without answering that question for herself. "I-I want..."

"There's no wrong answer." His voice was so deep and soothing, so gentle in the quiet.

"I want you to taste me," she admitted as heat suffused her skin. "I want you to touch me all over and then lick me. And then..." She opened her eyes and made herself meet his gaze. "And then I want you to take me. Hard and fast, not like you have to protect me but like you want to...to mark me. That's what I want."

His pupils had dilated with every word she said, and now he loomed over her, suddenly bigger and darker and stronger. He rubbed his hands down her bare sides until he hooked his fingers beneath what remained of her dress. He tugged and it fell away. Then he swept her up and deposited her on the bed.

She had barely positioned herself on his pillows when he began doing exactly what she asked. His hands cascaded down her body and his tongue followed. He sucked and nipped, he squeezed and teased. Her body lit on fire with every touch, and she opened her legs wider as he wedged himself there.

He peeled her open, grunting at the sight of her, already wet and ready for him. He bent his head and licked her, while at the same time he glided a finger inside. As he sucked and stroked with his tongue, he added a second finger, a third, and she lifted to his thrusts and gave herself over to sensation.

The world and all its confusion drifted away as she met his rhythm, bearing down on him with every thrust of his fingers and sweep of his tongue. He focused his mouth on her clitoris at last, sucking her hard enough that stars exploded in her vision. She dug her fingers into his hair, holding him there as she writhed to find her pleasure.

When she did, it was explosive. She rocked against him, gasping and moaning and riding the wave of pleasure that felt more like a tidal force that could wash everything away. Just as the orgasm faded, he dragged himself up her body, nipping with his teeth, soothing with his tongue. He took her mouth, letting her taste her release as he positioned himself at her sex.

"Emily," he whispered. "Look at me."

She forced herself to follow the order. He was so close that meeting his eyes felt like locking herself to him. Joining with him in a deeper way than just being taken by him.

"I have already marked you," he murmured as he slid into her in one smooth thrust. "You are marked and that will never change."

He thrust again, harder. "Because no matter what happens, you will think of these nights we shared."

Harder and faster now as she lifted to meet him, pleasure rising in her all over again. "You will dream of my cock in you, Emily. You will dream of my fingers and my tongue."

She began to gasp for air as he ground hard and thrust harder.

"And when you look at me, you'll know I know that. It will be the secret you cannot keep. Not from me."

She came as he kept talking, kept telling her about the wicked secret they would both know. The words didn't matter. She felt the truth in her bones rather than in her ears.

He was pounding harder and harder as he whispered those things in her ear, and just as her orgasm faded, he reared up and came, the heat of him splashing across her belly and her breasts. Their eyes held again and he reached down as if to wipe himself away. She caught his wrist and let him watch as she instead rubbed his essence into her skin.

"Bloody hell, Emily," he grunted as he flopped down beside her and dragged her to rest her head against his shoulder. For a little while they were quiet together, the only sound the occasional crackle of the fire.

"Why did you bring up the topic of my future marriage?" he asked.

She rested a hand on his chest, feeling his heart there. Comforted by the steady thud. "The topic has come up several times during our time here," she admitted. "By more than one lady. There are some who believe this Season will be the one you begin taking your search for a bride more seriously."

She felt him stiffen slightly, and then he let out a long sigh. "It may be true."

Four words. Simple on their surface. Not said cruelly or with any meaning that could be taken as such. And yet they stabbed her heart in a way she couldn't fully express. Certainly she couldn't have explained the sensation.

"My grandfather and my uncle have been patient these last few years," he continued. "But they have expectations. They will not force me to marry...yet. Though if I refuse to walk the path that has been laid out for me, I suppose they might. I admit I'm surprised to hear this rumor has been circulating."

She began to trace small circles against the muscles of his chest. His heart rate increased as she did so. "You are a catch," she said at last. "Diamonds and mamas will be on the hunt for you if there is even an inkling you might be open to the idea. They'll create a scenario where you are, even if you think you're not."

"I suppose so," he said, and he suddenly sounded tired. She glanced up and found him frowning toward the fire, his mind clearly taking him away from her.

She cleared her throat. "Have you...have you thought of who you might...consider?"

That brought his attention back, sharp and sudden and harder than any look he'd ever given to her. "Don't lie naked in my arms, in my bed, and try to matchmake me, Emily." He shook his head. "*Don't.*"

Her eyes went wide at that stern admonishment, said in a tone that seemed to spark in her bloodstream. Before she could respond, he caught her elbows and dragged her up his body. His mouth took hers, harder than before, more insistent as he positioned her still ready body over his rapidly hardening one.

He claimed her in one angry thrust, then he caught her backside and began to grind her over him as he continued those claiming, forceful kisses that swept her away and woke things in her she never would have thought were possible.

But as she surrendered to them, her last thought was still of the idea that Cav would marry. Someone, anyone. And then things would change even more so than they had when they became lovers.

And that terrified her.

CHAPTER 12

ELEVEN LADIES DANCING

Three days had passed since that troubling afternoon in Cav's bed. They'd been filled with maids milking (and flirting shamelessly, which had distracted the gentlemen of the party considerably), drummers drumming (far more headache-inducing than Emily had imagined) and pipers piping. (It turned out one could only tolerate one or two piped musical selections before one wished to run screaming from the room. Only those of Scottish descent had truly enjoyed *that* three-hour extravaganza.)

None of the events had seemed to push her guests closer together, either. Her matches were lackluster at best. Hostile at worst.

The party was turning into a disappointment all around. And that had only been magnified by the growing strain between her and Cav. *She* had been the one to make the rules of their affair, but every moment that passed, she struggled with them.

She didn't know how to be with him anymore when she wasn't curled in his bed, giving and receiving pleasure that seemed to wash away plans and reason and everything else but him and his hands and mouth and cock. That was what she thought of night and day, even when they were standing in a parlor, surrounded by people who couldn't ever discover the truth of what they were doing.

Meanwhile, Cav seemed perfectly fine. For all the desperation and passion he brought to her body in his chamber, once outside those four precious walls, he acted exactly the same as he always had toward her. He joked and played and escorted and danced and smiled all while she felt the grate of desire down her spine from just standing too close to him.

Of course, he had more practice in separating heart from body. He could not care at all and still derive pleasure. That was what rakes did, after all. In truth, she was likely just another warm body in his bed. Pleasure explored, but eventually forgotten in the warm glow of every other woman he'd derived it from.

For her it was more complicated. Sometimes she felt confused, as though she cared for Cav on a deeper level than mere friendship. As though she could even...*love* him.

But that couldn't be. It was only that she'd never bedded a man she didn't love. Andrew was her only point of reference.

"You look beautiful, my lady."

Emily started because she had gotten so wrapped up in thoughts of Cav that she had lost track of what her maid, Mary, had been doing as she readied her for the night's Epiphany Eve masquerade ball. This gathering would be larger than any of the others, and included many who hadn't been part of the country party.

Mary motioned toward the mirror, and Emily looked. She did look nice. She wore a new gown, one with fine beading and perfect gathering that created a waterfall of silk down the front of her dress. The sea-blue color matched her eyes perfectly. Cav liked gowns that did that. He always complimented her on them.

Drat. There she was, thinking of him again. She'd had the dress designed months ago with this ball in mind. She *couldn't* have been thinking of what Cav would want then...could she?

"My lady, do you not like what I've done with your hair?" Mary asked, her brow wrinkling in concern.

"I do," Emily assured her with a forced smile. She looked at her hair. Mary had curled and lifted and pinned it into a gorgeous swath of gold. "I love it—you are wonderful, as always. Now, shall we place the mask?"

Mary nodded and drew forth the most beautiful mask. To match her blue dress, Emily had it designed with peacock feathers and paste sapphires. Her smile widened to something more genuine as Mary settled it carefully so it wouldn't muss her hair.

She looked herself and yet not at the same time. A mysterious lady who could pretend to be anyone and anything else she wished to be. What would she do with that freedom? If she were someone else what...and *who*...would she pursue at a masquerade ball where a lady could be...naughty?

She feared she knew the answer to that question. Feared the thrill that worked through her at the idea. Cav kept returning to her mind, it seemed. Despite the fact that she knew their friendship was the most important thing. Despite the fact she already felt she was destroying it every time she inched closer to him.

She glanced at the clock and gasped. "Oh, gracious, I'm a little more than fashionably late. Thank you again, my dear."

"Have a wonderful evening, my lady," Mary called out as Emily dashed from the room.

She hurried down the stairs and through the halls to the ballroom. Already she heard music playing and imagined far more than eleven ladies were dancing inside, to thwart her Twelve Days of Christmas theme. She walked through the open doors and couldn't hold back her gasp.

Her staff had certainly earned the bonuses they would be receiving tomorrow for Epiphany. They had always taken wonderful care of her and tonight was no different. Her ballroom looked like a magical fairyland, with candlelight sparkling and pale blue gauze draped just so. Her staff wore plain white masks studded in gold and moved effortlessly through the crowd. They tended to guests, making everything so perfect that Emily's eyes filled with tears.

This was likely the last event she would ever host here. The last time she would be the lady of this house.

"My lady!"

She jolted from her maudlin thoughts and laughed as she was approached by some of her guests. Not only were her houseguests in attendance, but she had called forward friends from London and the shire, as well. It was a jolly, full ballroom, indeed.

She fell into the role of hostess, complimenting all the beautiful gowns and masks, playing the game of guessing who was who as she went from person to person. She almost felt herself again as she did so.

Almost. Because she still found herself glancing around the room whenever she had a moment. She could pretend a thousand reasons for that, but there was only one that was true: she was looking for Cav.

She found him after what felt like forever and recognized him instantly despite the fact that this was a masquerade. Good Lord, but he did look handsome. Everything he wore was fitted perfectly against that body she now knew as intimately as she knew his smile or his laugh. Buff trousers, shiny boots, a fine waistcoat threaded with gold and blue that somehow matched her own dress and hair perfectly. Like they'd planned it when of course they hadn't.

He glanced toward her as the crowd ebbed and flowed around them, and then he was moving toward her. Her heart leapt as she watched him weave in and out, but always driven to her. She wanted him so desperately in that moment. And she wanted so desperately to keep the feelings in her chest limited to mere desire.

"Would you care to dance, my lady?" he asked as he reached her. He held out a hand and she shivered. He wasn't wearing gloves, flouting propriety as he sometimes did.

She took his hand, her stomach fluttering at the warmth of him even through her own gloves. He guided her to the dancefloor and they fell into the turns of the waltz as the orchestra began.

He smiled at her. "And how is your evening so far, my lady?"

She wrinkled her brow. Did he not recognize her? Had he just come across the room and picked her without purpose? She was just another lady in the crowd who caught his rakish attention?

"Cav, you...you know who I am, don't you?" she asked.

His fingers tightened against her hip slightly, possessive, hungry, awakening a fire in her that she just couldn't seem to extinguish now. "Of course. Do you really think I wouldn't know you no matter what?"

"A masquerade is meant to trick the eye," she said, trying to keep her tone light.

He shook his head slowly. "Emily, I would know you in the dark of a moonless night. I would know you from a far distance without aid of a spyglass. I would know you in any costume, in any era."

"H-how?" she whispered. She shouldn't ask the question. The answer was too dangerous and she knew it. But she couldn't help herself.

I couldn't help myself. After the last eleven days, she really ought to needlepoint that onto a handkerchief and carry it with her as a cautionary tale.

"I know you from the way you catch your breath or say my name or turn your head. I know you."

His lips were curved in the little smile that was natural to him, but his dark blue eyes held hers without wavering and there was an intensity there that burned down deep into her soul. Made the rest of the room fade away, and suddenly it was as if they were back upstairs in his room, in his bed, all alone except for the walls she put between them in an attempt to not let this go too far.

But she could see now that it was too late. It was too far already. It had been too far from the first moment he kissed her.

She was shaking, but he kept her upright, just as he had for so long and through so much. She clung to him even though *he* was the storm that was lashing against her boat.

The music was fading now. A few more turns were all she had to stay on her feet. His smile fell away as he searched her face, and she knew he would see through her because he always did. Always had. Always would.

"Emily," he said softly.

She shook her head as the music ended at last. She executed a polite curtsey so prying eyes wouldn't see anything untoward.

"Please don't," she whispered as she pulled away from him.

He didn't repeat her name—for that she was happy. Not only would it draw that unwanted attention, but right now she felt like a string was connecting them and if he said her name she wasn't sure what would happen. Would it snap and separate them forever? Would she trip over it, wreaking havoc in her wake?

She didn't want to know. Not now. Not yet. Now when her entire life seemed to be slowly turning upside down and she just wanted to find a way to stay upright for a little longer.

She did it by pretending everything was fine as she made her way out of the ballroom. She waved to friends and spoke to servants and hoped she looked steady until she exited the ballroom with a great gasp of air.

She did not want these feelings that rose up in her chest, powerful and harsh. She didn't *want* the confusion and guilt and thrill that they brought with them. And she certainly didn't want to experience them as she stood in the middle of her late husband's ballroom with friends surrounding her, watching her every move.

A few partygoers approached the ballroom from the direction of the retiring area. Despite the masks, she recognized one of them as Lady Abigail. A woman Cav had seemed to show some interest in. Jealousy rushed back through her instantly, and she pivoted away.

She needed to not be here until she could gather herself and act like the rational adult she was. She staggered down the hall in the opposite direction. She wasn't thinking, she wasn't making logical decisions, she was just...*running*. Perhaps not physically, but in every other way one could do that.

She turned and threw open a door without thinking. As she entered the chamber, she stopped. She'd blindly made her way to the library. The place where Cav had first kissed her days before and unleashed this torrent of unexpected feelings and experiences.

Why had she come here, of all places, in this big house?

But she didn't leave the room. Instead she stepped inside and moved to the very spot she'd been standing when he kissed her that afternoon a lifetime ago. She shut her eyes and she could picture it now. See the tension coiled in his body as he tried to protect her from what would be unleashed if she allowed it.

Did she regret what they'd done? Right now, when she felt spun upside down, did she wish she had walked away instead of lifted her mouth in offering to him?

"No," she said out loud. And she meant it. She didn't regret one moment. When she thought of the alternative…of not experiencing all the pleasure he had given her, she could not wish things had been different.

"Emily."

She didn't open her eyes for a moment even as she heard Cav's voice say her name. Even as she heard him quietly shut the door behind him.

He was here. Of course he was here. He was always *here*, wherever here was, when she was weak or weary or unsteady.

"You are upset," he said softly, gently, like he was approaching a spooked mare. "I have not seen you so pale in a very long time. If I've caused you grief, please let me help. What is it?"

She opened her eyes at last and forced herself to look at him. She had looked at him so many times, in so many lights and ways, and he had never been so handsome as he was in that moment. His mask covered half his face, but his dark blue eyes still mesmerized. His well-defined jaw had been freshly shaven for the ball, and she longed to cup it, trace the line there, brush her own cheek against it. His hands, so strong and big but also so gentle, were gripped against his sides as he awaited her answer to his question. He leaned forward slightly, like a bull ready to charge forward toward her, catch her if she were to falter.

"Emily," he repeated. "You are frightening me."

She swallowed. "I-I can't do this, Cav. I'm not...like you. I can't turn off desire or emotion back and forth from one room to the next. I'm apparently incapable of not connecting my body to my—" She cut herself off and dropped her gaze from his. "—to anything else."

His eyes went wide as he stared at her for a beat, for two. Then he reached up and tugged the mask from his face. He tossed it aside in frustration and took a long step toward her. "Is that what you think I do? Separate my emotions from my body?"

She was breathless now that he was so close. Just the flutter of her hand and she could touch him. Kiss him. Ruin everything once and for all.

"That is what rakes do, is it not?" she asked. "You must be practiced in it, for you do it so well."

"No," he said, his voice suddenly low and dangerous. "I'm not. What I am practiced in, Emily, is tying them together and then hiding it so that no one will ever see. *You* will never see. I'm *practiced* at loving you and knowing you will never love me in return."

Her mouth dropped open and her ears began to ring, her arms tingle.

His face was a mask of pain, frustration gone and replaced by the pure truth she had never understood, never seen, never allowed herself to accept.

"I...I love you," he repeated.

CHAPTER 13

C av had never intended to make his confession tonight, here in the library where they'd begun it all. But a few words from her and he'd had no choice. The feelings that had burned within his heart for nearly a decade had fallen from his lips, and now they hung between them.

Emily's eyes shone with tears beneath her beautiful mask, her mouth dropped open with shock at what he'd told her.

"Please say something," he whispered.

She swallowed hard and backed toward one of the chairs in front of the fire. She sat down hard and stared up at him. "You are...in love with me?"

He nodded. "Yes."

"How...long have you felt this way?" she asked. Her voice broke as she said it.

He shifted because he knew the truth would hurt her, perhaps even anger her. Despite that, he couldn't lie. He'd spent too many years doing that already. "Emily—"

"*How long?*" she repeated, her tone louder and sharper.

He paced the bookshelf and fiddled with the spines a moment as he tried to find the courage for what would come next. The courage to face what he'd always allowed himself to hide away from.

He turned toward her slowly. "From the first moment I met you. Nine years ago."

"Cav," she said, and the way she gripped the armrests of the chair spoke volumes. She shook her head over and over, and finally she asked, "Did he know?"

They both knew who *he* was. There was no need for clarification.

"No," he said immediately. "I would never have told him that—it would have served nothing but to hurt him, hurt you. You were his. He loved you and you loved him. And I...I loved you both."

She lifted her hand and covered her mouth, and now her entire face was a mask. Only her wide eyes told him anything about her feelings.

"I sat back," he continued, "And never would have ever interfered. Even after he died—"

"Cav!" she burst out as she leapt to her feet.

"—you needed me as a friend," he continued. "And I wanted to be that for you. Truth be told, I needed you too. Only *we* understood that loss, didn't we? Only we knew what the other felt or needed in those horrible months and years after he was gone."

Her breath hiccupped from her mouth and she gasped, "Yes."

He shrugged. "So I still said nothing, all this time. For the same reasons you gave when you resisted coming to my bed. Neither of us wanted to damage what we had. Because it is important and precious and everything to me. But make no mistake, Emily: I love you."

She turned away and paced to the window. She stood there, shoulders rolled forward as she stared out at the dark night for what felt like a lifetime. She didn't face him as she said, "I-I don't know what to say."

He smiled at that. As terrifying as it was to wait for her reaction, as much as he feared that she would pull away, he felt lighter than he had in so long. Because the truth was out. He was no longer in hiding. He was free.

"I know you don't," he said. "Because you didn't see." Now she did face him with another soft gasp. He held up his hands in a gesture of understanding. "It's not an accusation, Em. I never expected you to see. I did everything in my power to keep you in the dark."

Her cheek twitched. "Then why...why tell me now?"

She wanted to close Pandora's Box. He understood that. How many years had he longed for the same before he finally accepted that his heart would not change? That he had to embrace the pain, and then he could feel the beauty of loving her, whether she ever returned that emotion or not.

"Because since we came here, since we kissed in this very room, in the very spot where you stood when I found you here tonight, we have connected. I *know* you feel it, even if you would deny it out of fear or self-preservation or guilt or a million other emotions I see playing over that beautiful face, mask or no mask."

"Because you would know me in the dark," she said, her voice a sob.

He smiled because she was quoting his words on the dancefloor back to him. Giving him wild hope he clung to with both hands, knowing it might slip away like so much sand in an hourglass.

But at least he'd know he'd tried. At least he wouldn't lay awake at night ever again, recognizing he was too cowardly to cross that invisible line that separated them.

"I would," he said. "This is beyond sex for you. If it weren't you wouldn't be jealous."

Now she gasped and it was with an affronted tone. "I am not jealous!"

He arched a brow. "Best friends, remember?" She folded her arms and glared at him. "And if it were just sex, I don't think you'd be pacing around the library, your lips pale. That wonderful mind of yours turning as it does when you are trying to think your way out of something."

"I would really like to hate you for knowing me so well. It's abominable in this situation," she said.

Relief flooded him. She was teasing with him, at least a little. Like old times. One more point for wild hope. "Hate away, I can take it."

She stepped toward him, but not close enough to touch. "I'm so confused, Cav."

He nodded. "And I know that, too. Understand, I don't expect you to have any answers right now. I've had nearly a decade to adjust to the fact that you are the center of my world. The love of my life."

"Cavendish," she whispered, her voice trembling at those words. "What would you have me do with this information, then? You imply you are the expert of the two of us. Advise me."

He moved toward her and caught her hand. He lifted it to his lips and kissed her gloved knuckles gently. Her fingers flexed against his. "I only ask you to think about what I've said to you tonight. Please consider it. Consider if it is something you could accept. Perhaps embrace? Consider if it is a feeling you could ever...return."

Her lips trembled. "And what if I can't?"

It felt like the air went out of the room with those words. He was no fool. He had studied this woman and examined his own heart for so long it was second nature to do so. He'd always known that revealing himself would be a risk. And that she might refuse him, either out of lack of feeling, or inability to accept for fear or guilt.

He drew a few long breaths to refill his lungs. To calm his racing heart. To keep himself from gripping her to him and proving she felt something with a kiss or by making love to her.

That wasn't fair.

"If you could not allow me into your heart, I would always be your friend, Emily. That will never change between us, love or not."

"Then you'll just continue to love me from afar forever?" she gasped. "That sounds almost unbearably cruel."

"Life is cruel, love. And sometimes it's not. I've lived with both and so have you." He released her hand. "I cannot imagine a scenario where I would not love you. Trust me, I tried very hard to change my heart at the beginning and could not. But..."

She swallowed. "But?"

He shook his head. "I will move on if you refuse me. I will have to do so—we've already talked about that."

"Marry, you mean," she said, her voice so soft it almost didn't carry despite how close they stood now.

"Yes, I mean I will marry. And I will have to live my life so I can be happy and not make anyone else in my path miserable."

She nodded slowly. "I understand."

He let out a sigh. Suddenly he was completely exhausted. Apparently letting go of a secret one had held for a third of one's life was so cathartic as to make a man dramatically take to his bed. "You'll need space now. So I'll go up. I won't ruin the rest of your beautiful party by putting myself in your way."

She caught her breath, and he could see she wished to talk him into pretending things were normal. He held up a hand to stop her. "And *I* need some of that space myself to think about what happened tonight, too."

He stepped closer to her. She didn't back away. He traced her cheek with his fingertips, let his thumb press to her lower lip. She tilted her face up, just as she had the first time he kissed her, and she was an undeniable temptation. He leaned into her and took her lips.

He wanted to devour her. He always wanted to do that. To press her as close as he could because he'd been forced to keep her so far for so long. But tonight he remained gentle. Not quite chaste, but not driven.

Her hands found his forearms, and she clung to him, her groan soft against his lips. When he stepped away at last, her gaze was blurry and dilated with desire.

"Think about it," he asked again.

She nodded. "I-I will think of nothing but."

He turned from her and left the room. As he headed for his chamber, his knees shook like a green boy who had just discovered his first object of desire. If he lost her, he knew how broken that would make him. The last decade of unspoken and unrequited love would be nothing compared to that moment of refused love. But at least he had put his cards on the table.

At least he finally had something to hope for. And so hope he would. For as long as she needed to think about what was, what had been and what could be if her heart could open.

~

E mily dropped both her hands against the back of the chair as Cav left the room, and leaned there with all her weight. She drew in ragged breaths one after another as the tremor of what had just happened ripped through her body and her heart and her every belief.

Cav loved her.

That fact hung like a weight around her neck and she drooped beneath it. "Nine years," she breathed. "How could I have been so blind for *nine* years?"

"My lady?" She jolted at the sound of Cringle's voice behind her and turned to find the butler standing at the doorway. "I am sorry to disturb, Lady Rutledge, but we are running short on wine. Would you like me open a case of madeira?"

For a moment, Emily had the wild desire to laugh. After all, she had just been hit by a lightning bolt, but here the world was...still turning. Wine drunk, jigs danced, servants waited as if the rug hadn't been pulled straight out from beneath her.

"Would two cases be better?" she asked with a smile for her butler as she crossed to the door and motioned him to follow her into the hall. They walked back toward the ballroom together.

"I think they will be drunk if they are opened," he said.

"Then do so," she said. "Thank you."

He gave a low bow and moved off to fulfill that duty, and Emily stared into the ballroom from the distance. The party was in full swing. And as much as she wished to go hide in her chamber and digest Cav's confession, this was where she needed to be.

So she drew a long breath and entered the room. She had not made it three steps inside when Lord Allington approached. The earl was very handsome in his dark attire and mask adorned with crow's feathers.

"There you are, Lady Rutledge," he said as he sidled up to her. "I was told you were wearing a peacock mask, and it is delightful."

She smiled up at him. "And you a devious crow."

"I was inspired by Cavendish's recital of Jago's 'The Blackbirds' a week back."

Emily had to fight to keep her smile on her face. Cav's reading of that poem had led to so much. It said so much about him and how he always stepped up to protect her.

"It was...inspiring," she managed to croak out.

"Yes, birds of a feather and all. Where is the man, anyway?" Allington looked around, past her toward the hall.

She swallowed. "You are asking me?"

"Well, you two are friends. Wherever one is, the other seems sure to follow," Allington said.

Emily could not deny that. She didn't *want* to deny it. Her friendship with Cav was the most important of her life. Many didn't understand it. They couldn't picture a friendship between a man and a woman that didn't involve something more.

But of course, their friendship always *had* involved something more. She just had been blind to it until the moment he kissed her.

"Lady Rutledge?"

She blinked as she realized her distraction was causing Allington to look at her far more closely than she wished to be examined. "I did see Cavendish," she admitted. "He complained of a slight headache and excused himself."

"Ah." For a moment Allington shifted and seemed truly troubled by the fact that he could not speak to Cav. But then he flashed her a grin and the worry seemed gone from his countenance...or at least the part she could see. "Well, we'll just have to make a party without him, won't we? Would you care to dance, Lady Rutledge?"

Emily nodded, for there was no way to refuse. Perhaps it would give her racing mind a rest. So she took to the floor and danced. She put on a show for her party until long after midnight.

And all the while she screamed inside, thinking of what Cav had told her. Running over and over the look on his face when he'd admitted his heart. And wondering what in the world she should do... how she should respond when everything felt so important and close.

She would have to decide soon. Cav had, apparently, been waiting a long time. And the longer this hung between them, the more she feared it would grow into a wall she could not surmount. And *that* would be a tragedy.

CHAPTER 14

TWELVE FIDDLERS FIDDLING

"I t has been a good party."

Emily jolted as Lady Hickson slipped up beside her, and they stood together, watching the fiddlers play at the final official gathering of the season. The party had gone to Epiphany services together a few hours before. For some they seemed far too early after such a ball the night before. Gifts had been exchanged, games played, and now the group sat quietly, listening to the music, talking to each other softly.

An anticlimactic end to what she had hoped to achieve here. And to what had actually happened within these walls.

Her gaze slipped to Cav. He was sitting all the way across the music room from her. Twenty steps or less, but it felt like an insurmountable distance. He smiled at her and lifted a glass in mock toast.

Perhaps that should have put her at ease, that friendly little look he'd given her a thousand times, but it somehow didn't. She still had no idea how to feel, what to do, what to say to him. And at any rate, the smile didn't reach his eyes. Not anymore.

"My lady?"

Emily started as she realized she had not yet responded to Lady Hickson. "Yes, very nice," she managed weakly as Cav looked away.

Lady Hickson wrinkled her brow. "You don't sound very convincing."

Emily bowed her head as heat flooded her cheeks. "I apologize. I don't think I'm much good company at present."

Lady Hickson caught her arm and drew her farther from the crowd. Her expression was seeking and worried. *"Emily."* She accentuated Emily's given name. "You and I have only been passing friends over the years, but I have made an observation of you in that time. You've seemed...troubled since the ball last night."

Emily shut her eyes briefly. Since Cav's confession. She'd tried so hard to not let anyone else see her feelings, but clearly she had failed. But how could she not? To know what was in his heart...what had been in his heart for their entire friendship...

It had changed her irrevocably.

Virginia was still talking. "Since you've been so kind as to include me here, to offer me kindness at a time of year that is usually difficult for me, might I offer you some of the same in return?"

"How?" Emily croaked. "How could you help me?"

Virginia squeezed her arm. "I could offer an ear, if you need it. A talk, widow to widow."

Emily shifted and her gaze returned to Cav. She did so desperately need to speak about what had happened. Just to say it out loud in the hopes it would stop repeating in her head over and over and over again. "I-I normally speak to *him* about my troubles."

Virginia followed her gaze and her eyes went a little wider. "Ah, I see. Am I to assume that *he* is your trouble now?"

Emily glanced at her. Virginia had never been anything but kind to her. She was not known as a gossip. Perhaps this was a risk she could take. *Needed* to take.

"What I'm about to tell you is intensely private," she whispered. "May I count on you to keep your counsel?"

Virginia held her stare. "I swear to you on the soul of my dearly departed mama, whatever you say shall never find any other ears from me."

"Things between Cavendish and me have...shifted here," she admitted, and felt her cheeks burn with the intimacy of what she was saying.

Virginia swallowed. "*Shifted.* What do you mean?" Emily worried her lip and raised both eyebrows gently. Now it was Virginia's turn to blush. "Are you speaking of...physically?"

"Yes," Emily whispered. "I'm speaking of *exactly* what you think."

"Oh my," Virginia gasped. "I thought you two were only friends, despite some murmurings to the contrary."

"We always were friends until..." Emily let out a long sigh and then leaned closer to whisper the story to Virginia. Of the affair. Of Cav's confession of a decade of secret love. And when she was finished, Virginia looked as shocked as she, herself, felt.

"So for nine years..." she breathed.

Emily nodded. "Yes. So he says."

"And you didn't know? That is like something out of a book!"

Emily hesitated. It *did* seem like something out of one of her beloved novels. The ones she read out to Cav in the winter when he came to call. He'd lounge on her chaise, eyes closed, a contented smile on his handsome face. And afterward they'd eat supper together and discuss whatever latest adventures had been had in the pages. She shook the thought away.

"I didn't *see*," Emily said. "But now all I can do is see. And recognize how the signs of his feelings were before me all along."

"What do you mean?"

Emily glanced across the room at him again. Cav was talking to Allington, now. His expression was serious. It was so rarely serious that it made her catch her breath.

"All the times he looked at me, smiled at me from across a room like this. All the times he sat with me, the only one who didn't tell me I must stop crying or overcome my grief after Andrew was gone. All the times he cried right along with me. All the times he teased me or encouraged me or supported me...I realize now *all* of those were his declarations of love."

Virginia blinked, and there were tears in her eyes that matched the sting in Emily's. "But what about *you?*"

"Me?"

"You two have always been thick as thieves," Virginia said. "What about all the times you did the same things you've described Mr. Cavendish doing?"

Emily bent her head. She'd been so focused on Cav that she'd been ignoring her own heart. Perhaps because exploring that heart would lead to a response to what he'd told her. Something that would change things between them, no matter what she decided about the future.

But that was unfair to him. Unfair to herself. At some point she had to stop being a coward.

"At first my responses to him were truly only in friendship," she said. "But I suppose, when I think about it, when I truly consider the last few years especially..." She trailed off. "Oh, Virginia, I don't know what we've shared, what I've done is anymore. Or was. Or what it could be. I'm just so confused because now it's all colored by what he has said."

Virginia caught her hands. "Hush now, don't get upset. How you feel is completely understandable. It's a great deal to think about."

"It is so much," Emily agreed. "What he has told me could change everything in my life. *Everything* in my future. It has already changed our friendship, our connection."

Virginia squeezed her hands gently. "May I make a suggestion?"

Emily nodded. "I would take any I can get at this point. Please, help me!"

Virginia smiled at her. "Don't rush this."

"But—" Emily began.

Virginia laughed. "I can see that is an anathema to you. You seem the sort of person who likes to have an answer right away."

"Yes. I've always gone with my instincts when it comes to what to do." Emily huffed out a breath. "I plan parties with birds as the centerpiece within weeks, I change my hair on a whim, I don't know what I want until the exact moment I want it. How can a person like me come up with an answer for a man who has...plodded along with his affection for a third of his life? He's been *pondering* this, Virginia, if you can imagine such a thing."

Virginia's laughter continued. "The fact that you can tease about it is a good thing. But that vital part of your personality, that impulsiveness that makes you so much fun to be around...I'm not sure that is the right answer here. Mr. Cavendish was right when he said he's had *years* to understand his heart. To come to grips with these emotions that now bubble between you two. You have had what...just a bit more than twelve hours?"

Emily glanced at the clock. "Fifteen hours, twelve minutes...give or take a few seconds."

"Then I do not think that asking him for a few days, at a minimum, is expecting too much."

"No," Emily agreed. "And he would never demand me to do what I wasn't ready to do. He never has, has he?"

"It seems not. So take the gift he's giving you, the time he's giving you, and truly consider what *you* want. Not what you think you should want. Not what *he* wants. Not what could happen or not happen no matter what decision you come to." She squeezed her hands. "Emily, this is your heart, your future. It shouldn't be considered lightly."

"When I met Andrew, it was a lightning bolt for both of us," Emily said with a sad smile, for she could no longer maintain the playfulness when it came to this subject. "I knew and he knew and everything fell into place perfectly. In this situation, there is so much more to determine. I *must* take the time and be more deliberative than my heart would perhaps like to be, I know you're right."

"I *am*." Virginia glanced off toward Cav.

Emily followed her gaze. He was in profile now, standing with a handful of the men in attendance. He smiled and her heart fluttered.

"Do consider this, though, along with all the rest," Virginia continued. "You were a lucky woman to marry one love of your life. Many in our circles don't even get that. But to have two? That would make you charmed, indeed."

Emily pursed her lips. "It is nothing to dismiss out of hand."

"Indeed, it is not."

Emily let out her breath in a long sigh. "I think I must speak to him. Let him know I'm going to take some time after the party, so he'll stop jumping every time I look at him sideways."

"Is he jumping?" Virginia said with a laugh. "He seems steady enough to me."

"Yes, but I know his tells," Emily said.

Virginia nodded. "Of course you do."

Emily squeezed Virginia's hand lightly. "Thank you."

She heard Virginia's response as she walked away, but could not have repeated it back to anyone if asked. She was too focused on Cav now. Especially when his gaze fell to her and sent a ripple of response through her.

She could only hope he would understand her need for time. And that if she took enough of it, her tangled mind would find the answer she sought.

$\sim$

E mily was coming toward him. He felt that before he turned and saw it was true. She was weaving her way through the crowd, a nervous look on her face that made him just as wary of what was about to happen. But he fought to keep his own expression clear and forced a smile as she reached him.

"Emily," he said. "You and Lady Hickson seemed to be engrossed in important talk."

Emily glanced over her shoulder. Lady Hickson had moved back into the crowd and taken a seat beside Wentworth Highsmith to watch the musicale continue.

"Perhaps my matchmaking failed on the whole," Emily said. "But I think I have come out of this with a new and potentially very true friend. So I will count it as a success."

"Good," Cav said. "I hated to see you batter yourself over your plans."

She smiled at him. "Yes. You are always looking out for me, it seems. More so than I even realized."

He shifted, for the praise for what he thought of as a cowardly act was difficult to take. "I also protected myself, I fear."

"Why would you not?" she asked. "Don't judge yourself, either, Cav."

"Is that what you came across the room to tell me?" he asked.

She caught her breath and he could see her discomfort as plain as her eyes or her hair or her pretty green dress. "Could we...could we step onto the terrace a moment? I need a moment of privacy with you."

His hands shook, so he gripped them into fists to settle them as he said, "Of course. It's not as cold today."

They moved to the terrace doors and slipped outside together. Though it wasn't as chilly as it had been during the party, the afternoon air was still brisk. But he hardly noticed the discomfort as he stared at her.

"What do you need to say?" he asked, breathless.

She worried her hands in front of her. Clenching and unclenching, over and over. "Everyone is leaving tomorrow, back to London or parts farther flung. And I know you were supposed to stay for luncheon and make your way back to London in a caravan with me. But..." She shook her head. "I think it might be best if you left with the rest of the party."

All the blood left his limbs, and Cav had to clear his throat to find his voice. "I-I see. You do not wish me here anymore?"

"It isn't that," she gasped, and stepped toward him. "Cav, I realized today that since you confessed to me all I've thought about is you. What you think, what you've felt, what you want...and if I am to take this seriously, I'm going to have to take a much harder look at...at me.

What I feel. What I want. What I *need* from a future either with you or alone. And I won't be able to do that with you at my side, or even back in London together when I'll know you're just a quarter mile away."

His heart jumped. This did not seem to be the rejection he'd feared. At least not out of hand. "I see. Then what will you do?"

She looked around. "I'm going to stay here a while. I was going to come back in a week or so to make final arrangements for my personal effects anyway. This will give me the chance to do that and to have a more private goodbye with the servants who have served me so well this past decade." She blushed. "And to think about what you told me without...distractions."

He nodded. What she said made sense, of course. And he wanted her to have all the time she needed to make the best decision for herself.

But oh, how he wished that what she'd been calling him here to do was to throw herself into his arms. That it would be as easy for her as it had been for him on a long ago night that often felt like yesterday.

"I understand," he said with difficulty. "Do you...know how long you'll be?"

"A few days?" she said. "And I will write you when I return to London. But I may need even more time than that, Cav. I don't know. I don't want to mislead you on that score. Because I do care so very deeply for you."

He almost laughed. He had declared his love and she said she cared deeply. That stung when she meant it as a balm.

"I appreciate it," he choked out. "And I do understand. I hope you will find the answers you seek, Emily. You deserve them and to be able to make whatever decision is right for *you*." He stepped a little closer. "Because I want you to be happy, no matter what that looks like."

She shook her head slightly. "Yes. You've more than proven that, I think."

She shivered, and he shrugged away his troubles. "Now you're freezing. Let's go in. We won't speak of this again until you are ready to do so."

"Cav," she said as he turned toward the door.

He flinched as she said it. "Yes?"

"Thank you."

The words softened him, and he nodded before he motioned her back inside. And as they parted again, it felt a little more permanent. He could only hope that was a trick of his imagination and not the harbinger of things to come.

CHAPTER 15

C av nursed a drink as he watched his grandfather pace his parlor, eyes that looked so much like his own storming with every turn.

"Does she not know what a catch you are?" he snapped as he flopped himself down at last on Cav's settee and grabbed for the whisky Cav had poured him right before confessing the entire tale of what had happened at Emily's Christmas party.

The weight of it had become so much harder to bear as the days had passed, and then a week. She'd returned to London the night before, but he'd had no message from her yet. Just the rumors through their shared friends that she was home.

It did not bode well.

"I'm certain she's well aware of my financial and social benefits, yes," he said, his tone dry as the desert.

The marquess snapped his gaze to Cav's face. "That isn't what I mean at all."

"No?" Cav said as he sipped his own drink. "I cannot imagine what other advantages you think I could offer the lady."

His grandfather scooted to the front of the settee and draped his elbows over his knees. "I have watched you pine for this woman for well near a decade," he said softly. "Offering her everything she could ever want or need all while you remained silent about your own desires. She would be lucky to be loved by a man like you. She would be lucky to love you in return."

Cav smiled slightly. "You are not often prone to waxing poetic about emotions, old man. But I appreciate your thinking so highly of me. Also, I adore you too."

His grandfather grunted and glared at him, but Cav could see the twitch to his lips. The playfulness that had always existed even if they quarreled. At least he knew he would have his family at his side if everything went...wrong...with Emily.

Cav pushed to his feet. "I cannot be angry with her, though. I don't wish for you to be, either. After all, she has a right to her feelings, doesn't she? I cannot and would not ever force her to try to change her heart out of some sort of...obligation."

"But you are disappointed that she has left you hanging so long." A statement, not a question.

Cav bent his head, all pretense of playfulness gone. He could not tease, not about this. "I admit, I had some dream in my head that I would declare my heart and she would immediately confess to similar feelings. Or that within a day or two, she would recognize the joy we could bring to each other for the rest of our days. I would have liked it to be...easy...after so many years of battling my feelings."

His grandfather nodded and his expression had softened. "I would have liked that for you, too, Cavendish."

Cav sighed. "But all I can do now is wait, isn't it? And hope the cards fall in my direction."

"I suppose that is all you can—"

Before his grandfather could finish, the door to the parlor opened and Cav's butler, Jennings, stepped into the room. "Pardon the intrusion, Mr. Cavendish, my lord. You have a caller, but I wasn't certain if you would wish to receive her as you have a guest."

Cav blinked. The guest was a she. He exchanged a quick look with his grandfather as he rose to his feet and faced Jennings. There must have been a great deal reflected on his face, for the normally strait-laced butler seemed concerned for a brief moment.

"Who is it?" Cav asked, his voice barely carrying no matter how much he tried to make it seem strong and unaffected.

"Lady Rutledge, sir."

Cav reached back to steady himself on the chair he had abandoned. His legs suddenly felt like he'd been at sea and his vision blurred slightly.

"Emily is here," he repeated. "Well, please send her in. I would very much like to receive her."

As Jennings exited the room to fetch her, the marquess got to his feet and smoothed his jacket. Cav blinked, trying to bring his attention back to the room rather than focus only on Emily, Emily, Emily, Emily...

"I will say hello to the lady and then I shall leave you," his grandfather said.

Cav drew in a long breath. "I'm surprised you don't want to stay here and involve yourself."

"With this? No. But I do hope you will come and call on me and tell me good news," his grandfather said. Then he stopped talking as Jennings ushered Emily into the room.

"Lady Rutledge, Mr. Cavendish, Lord Comerford."

She stepped around him, her gaze finding Cav. Her eyes lit up and she smiled slightly, then she glanced toward his grandfather. "Oh, my lord," she said, breathless. "I did not realize you were also here. I apologize for interrupting you two, I ought to have made an appointment."

The marquess snorted as he came forward and caught both of Emily's hands in his as greeting. For all his bluster about her, Cav could see the genuine affection his grandfather felt toward her. "Posh, my dear, I think you already know you needn't have an appointment to call on my grandson. And I was just on my way out."

"Oh dear." Emily looked up at him. "I hope I haven't chased you away."

"Not at all," he assured her with a glance at Cav. "You look lovely, as always. A very happy new year to you, and Cav, I expect to hear from you soon."

Cav gave him a half-salute, and his grandfather snorted as he exited the room and pointedly closed the door behind himself. Which left them alone. At last. As usual. Only this time it didn't feel normal or friendly or anything but charged as Emily clasped her hands before herself and fiddled with her fingers restlessly.

"Good afternoon," she said at last.

He chuckled. "Good afternoon." There was a pause that lasted for what felt like an eternity and then he shook his head. "God's teeth, I hope we aren't going to stumble all over each other like this. Not after all we've been through. Would you like a drink? I have tea or whisky."

Her eyes went wide. "So early?"

"If it's after one, my grandfather believes it's not too early. And today I happened to agree. Tea then?" He moved to the sideboard and began to grab for a cup. Her favorite cup, of course.

She shifted. "The whisky isn't the worst idea."

He glanced at her over his shoulder. One more comment that didn't bode well for his heart. But he managed to keep his calm as he traded a teacup for a tumbler and poured her a finger of whisky and a finger of water, since he knew she didn't like it straight.

He handed it over, careful not to touch her as he did so. He feared if he did, this might become messier than it needed to be.

"Please, sit," he said softly. "I heard you got back to Town last night."

She arched a brow. "Our gossip circle has reported well. I did. I... stayed at Crossfox a few days longer. I needed the time."

He swallowed and watched her sip her drink, then down the entire thing in one gasping gulp. He did the same and set his glass aside. Liquid courage for what he was about to say.

"I've tried to be patient," he said. "I know you need your space, and perhaps it isn't fair, but I must know. What decision, if any, did you come to, Emily? About me. About us."

She pushed to her feet and walked across the room. At the fire, she turned and folded her arms. "Do you know how difficult all this has been?" she asked. "When I am struggling, I talk to you. When I'm hurting, I talk to you. When I'm confused, the only advice that ever makes any sense is…yours."

He was holding his breath and had to let it out to say, "Because we're friends."

She moved a little closer. "Because you are the most…" She caught her breath. "…the most important person in my life."

His hands shook as he slowly rose to his feet. "Emily," he whispered.

"When you told me you loved me, it frightened me down to my very core, Cav. Because I didn't want to lose you if this changed things too much. But as the hours passed, as the days passed, what you told me really sank in. The meaning of it became so very clear. You've been in love with me for years."

"I have," he said.

She shrugged. "And it hasn't changed *anything*. So I had to stop thinking about it from your side and start thinking about it from mine. *I'm* the one who will change everything or destroy everything. And it kept me longer while I pondered what that would mean."

He found difficulty making words as he stared at her. "And what did you decide, Emily, as you pondered your side of this? I don't think I can wait any longer to know. Please tell me what it is you've decided. Because I can see you've decided something."

"Of course you can," she said with a smiling shake of her head. "Of course you can. So I won't leave you waiting any longer."

E mily's words choked her but she fought to say them, just as she'd practiced all last night and during the walk over to his home from hers. But now that he was standing before her, it was hard to think of anything except just how handsome he was. And how much she wanted to take his hand.

But first she needed to say these things.

"If you cannot wait to see someone every time they're gone, if you miss them so much it hurts, if you think about them all the time... that's love, isn't it? It's all love."

She expected him to smile, to move toward her, to be joyful in her declaration. But instead his shoulders rolled forward a fraction and his brow wrinkled. "What you are describing...it could also be the love of friendship, Emily. Listen to me: I know you don't want to hurt me. You are too kind to do so. But I don't want you to talk yourself into loving me just to make me happy or to keep our friendship intact."

She stared at him. He looked so devastated at the thought, but also resigned. He was willing to let her go to make her happy. And that made her emotions swell all the higher.

"Oh dear, I'm making a mess of this. I've explained it all wrong," she muttered. "Let me try again. While I was at Crossfox this last week, I thought a great deal about how I've felt for you the last few years. I even went to Andrew's grave to talk to him about it."

His expression softened. "I did the same last week."

She smiled. "I'm glad of it. He was so important to me, Cav. I loved him very much and I will always love him. But the idea of being parted from you ever again, it is too painful for me to fathom. I thought of all our jokes and laughter. I thought of your support and mine to you. I thought of what it's like when I enter a room and find you there, already staring back at me. I thought of what it was like the first time you kissed me and it felt so...right, so perfect. I thought of when you made love to me and how much I want you, not just with my body, but down to my very soul."

She moved toward this man she had been pondering and considering and analyzing for days. She reached up at last, tracing his jawline with her fingertips. "I never want to be parted from you again, John Cavendish."

When she used his full name, his mouth fluttered a little. Like he was shocked. Like he was moved.

"I have loved you for a long time. Not as long as you've loved me. But for years. Even though I tried to ignore it, call it something else."

His eyes lit up, pure joy on a face that already gave her so much of the same.

"More importantly, I love you *today*. I will love you tomorrow. I will love you forever." She shifted because he was being so quiet as he stared at her. "If you'll have me."

"If I'll have you," he said, his arms coming around her waist and tugging her closer. "Can you really have doubt about that? If I am not reacting as strongly as you expected, it is because I am in shock and disbelief. Is this a dream, or did you really just tell me you love me?"

"Really," she whispered, and leaned up to brush her lips to his. "Madly." She kissed him deeper and his fingers bunched against her back. "Truly," she murmured against his tongue, and felt him smile. She pulled away. "Deeply. So very deeply."

Tears had sprung into his eyes, and she caught her breath at seeing them there. Not tears of loss or sorrow like they had shared so many times since Andrew's death. These were tears of joy. And suddenly the future felt very real and very bright and very close, indeed.

"Marry me," he said.

"Are you certain, so soon?"

"So soon?" he said with a bark of laughter. "So soon says the lady who makes decisions on a lark?"

"But I've been practicing patience over the last week," she said. "Perhaps I'll take to it."

"Never!" he said, his smile widening. "I refuse to accept it. And this isn't so soon for me. I've been in love with you forever, don't you recall?"

"Yes," she said.

"Yes you recall or yes you'll marry me?" he asked.

"Yes to both," she said without hesitation.

He caught her closer and lifted her from her feet as he spun her around the room. When he set her down, he cupped her cheeks and kissed her again, far more deeply and gently, and she melted against his chest in pure pleasure and true surrender. Because she was his.

He pulled back a fraction. "Run away with me to Gretna Green so we don't have to wait a moment more?"

"Yes to it all," she said. "Yes to everything forever..."

His laughter merged with hers on another kiss, and she laughed again at his ardor. At his certainty. At the future he offered so effortlessly and beautifully, and all the joy it would hold for the rest of her days.

EPILOGUE

One week later

"So you waited for nearly a decade and then you ran off to Gretna Green to marry the woman on a whim?"

Cav smiled, because though his grandfather was trying to sound stern, he looked as happy as Cav felt as they watched Emily flit around to their friends and family at this small celebration of their recent marriage. Including some of those who had been part of the Christmas gathering. Andrew's family was also there and seemed over the moon at the union of two who had been so dear to their fallen son and brother.

This was Cav's wife. *Emily* was his wife. He nearly staggered from the joy of that.

"I did," he said. "Because I could not wait a day longer."

His grandfather slung an arm around him. "And you are deliriously happy together, it seems."

Cav glanced at him. "I was not certain you entirely approved, though. Do you?"

"Not that it matters, because you have always done as you pleased," the marquess said. "But my only hesitation about the lady had to do with protecting your very vulnerable heart. But now...now I see her look at you with the same expression you always had for her. And I could not be more pleased with the union."

Emily had begun to approach as they talked, and she leaned up to kiss the marquess's cheek before she took Cav's hand. "I'm glad to hear it. I would not wish for the very intimidating Marquess of Comerford to disapprove my union with his grandson."

The marquess gave Cav a playful glare. "You are a bad influence on the lady, I fear."

"The very worst," Cav said as Emily guided him away from his grandfather and out onto the terrace.

The starry night was cold, but what was weather when they were so warmed by all the love between them? She leaned up to kiss him and he was lost, as always. Found, as always.

"Seems you are the worse influence, after all," he murmured as they parted. "Please do not tell the others or my reputation will be in tatters."

"I would never ruin your reputation," she teased as he wrapped an arm around her. "It was nice that Lady Hickson and some of the others from the party a few weeks ago came to celebrate."

"Yes. I may have destroyed the hopes of a few unmarried ladies, but none of them seem to judge me for being desperately and completely in love with you." She sighed. "I only wish I could have made them the matches I planned. Everyone should have the happiness I do now."

"Well they may find their happiness yet, love," he assured her.

She cuddled a little closer against his chest as they looked up at the night sky together.

A star streaked across the dark after a few moments, and they gasped together at the sight. He couldn't help but smile. "You are supposed to make a wish, I think, in such circumstances."

"We both know that isn't a star meant to grant a wish," she

breathed as she faced him. "But rather a message that we should be happy with the wishes that have already come true. I love you, Cav."

He cupped her cheek and ducked his head to take her lips again. "I love you, Emily. Always and forever."

ALSO BY JESS MICHAELS

Three Women. One Murdered Husband. Will *The Three Mrs* find love from a hopeless place? Coming in January 2021, a new series by 10-Time USA Today Bestselling Author Jess Michaels.

The Duke's By-Blows

The Love of a Libertine

The Heart of a Hellion

The Matter of a Marquess

The Redemption of a Rogue

The Shelley Sisters

A Reluctant Bride

A Reckless Runaway

A Counterfeit Courtesan

The Scandal Sheet

The Return of Lady Jane

Stealing the Duke

Lady No Says Yes

My Fair Viscount

Guarding the Countess

The House of Pleasure

The 1797 Club

The Daring Duke

Her Favorite Duke

The Broken Duke

The Silent Duke

The Duke of Nothing

The Undercover Duke

The Duke of Hearts

The Duke Who Lied

The Duke of Desire

The Last Duke

Seasons

An Affair in Winter

A Spring Deception

One Summer of Surrender

Adored in Autumn

The Wicked Woodleys

Forbidden

Deceived

Tempted

Ruined

Seduced

Fascinated

The Notorious Flynns

The Other Duke

The Scoundrel's Lover

The Widow Wager

No Gentleman for Georgina

A Marquis for Mary

To see a complete listing of Jess Michaels' titles, please visit:

http://www.authorjessmichaels.com/books

ABOUT THE AUTHOR

USA Today Bestselling author Jess Michaels likes geeky stuff, Vanilla Coke Zero, anything coconut, cheese, fluffy cats, smooth cats, any cats, many dogs and people who care about the welfare of their fellow humans. She is lucky enough to be married to her favorite person in the world and lives in the heart of Dallas, TX where she's trying to eat all the amazing food in the city.

When she's not obsessively checking her steps on Fitbit or trying out new flavors of Greek yogurt, she writes historical romances with smoking hot alpha males and sassy ladies who do anything but wait to get what they want. She has written for numerous publishers and is now fully indie and loving every moment of it (well, almost every moment).

Jess loves to hear from fans! So please feel free to contact her in any of the following ways (or carrier pigeon):

www.AuthorJessMichaels.com
Email: Jess@AuthorJessMichaels.com

Jess Michaels raffles a gift certificate EVERY month to members of her newsletter, so sign up on her website:
http://www.AuthorJessMichaels.com/

facebook.com/JessMichaelsBks
twitter.com/JessMichaelsBks
instagram.com/JessMichaelsBks
goodreads.com/JessMichaelsBks
bookbub.com/authors/jess-michaels